THESE WALLS DON'T TALK, THEY SCREAM

By

Kevin Holton

A HellBound Books Publishing LLC Book
Houston TX

A HellBound Books LLC Publication

www.hellboundbookspublishing.com

Printed in the United States of America

Dedication:

This book is for the ghosts that haunted my childhood home. I'm glad you and your cat found peace.

Also by Kevin Holton

At the Hands of Madness, from Severed Press.

Visions from the Veil, from River's End
Publications

Acknowledgements:

I owe thanks to a few people for this, but I'll keep it short. My eternal and humble thanks to Lisa Sofranko, for your tireless editorial eye and support of "my homie," as you were so fond of saying.

Thanks go out to my family, too, for supporting me during this (and all my other) projects, to Dylan "Nuclear Crab" Newman for your encouragement and great nicknames, and to the other publishers I've worked with along the way--Mighty Quill Books, Severed Press, and Siren's Call Publications. Validation is great inspiration.

Of course, thank you, friend, for reading. I hope you've enjoyed your time here.

THESE WALLS DON'T TALK, THEY SCREAM

Prologue

For five days, I have watched them going through the motions of their lives. The little one, the three-year-old, Charlotte, does what a kid like her should do: she eats when her parents tell her to, she watches goofy little shows on the TV, she likes to rub her face on the carpet when no one's there to stop her. Her mother, Darleen, lies about her age, usually saying 30, sometimes 28, so I don't know how old she is. Most of her day is spent doing yoga, cleaning the house, caring for Charlotte, or popping zits in the bathroom mirror, only to panic and cover the wounds with some kind of ointment, then a metric fuckload of cover-up. Her husband's name is George, and it's hard to get a read on him because he goes to work early, comes home late, eats dinner, tells Darleen about 'that idiot Steve' from the office and what nonsense he did that day, then reads Charlotte a bedtime story so she falls asleep early. If they aren't too tired, George and Darleen spend their remaining hours drinking wine on the back porch or desperately screwing in their basement with the quiet desperation of suburban parents who settled down too soon and didn't quite get all the thumping concert baselines and teenage wanderlust out of their system.

Of these five nights, Charlotte wet the bed once. Her parents didn't make a big deal out of it. George took care of it because "you spend all day looking after her, so let me take this." It's so damn cute, I could kill myself. But I'm not ready to try that yet. I've been trapped in the walls of their house for these past five days, and it's driving me a little crazy, but not *that* crazy.

There's plenty I can do to not get mind-crushingly bored. I have free reign of my prison, able to climb up and down to whatever floors I want, or scurry along the crawlspaces like a rat. They don't have rats, so that's nice. They do have termites. I've tried telling them. I've tried telling them *anything,* like how they keep tripping in the living room because the floors are sinking, or how the drainpipe to their kitchen sink is rotting out and causing damage, or how they have a human being stuck in their walls, but they can't hear me.

I'm actually not sure if I'm trapped in *their* walls, or some kind of weird pocket dimension that just mimics their house. I bang my fists, I scream, I stomp, but they don't hear me. If they do, they don't react. There are no exits, but that kind of makes sense. In most houses, you don't exactly have exposed panels, or sections where you can just casually reach behind the plaster. The crawlspaces were sealed up years ago, because this house, if Darleen was telling her friend Marjorie the truth, is over a hundred years old, and there's no point in having spaces like that anymore. They only collect dirt and pests and aren't useful to the homeowner.

After a day and a half in here, I tried punching my way out, tried kicking open the door to the crawlspace while Darleen was out with Charlotte at some kind of child painting class, but no luck. I heard the bang, but the walls didn't shake. The floor didn't rumble. I starred in a movie, the action playing out on screen with no physical impact. Two days later, I tried prying at the sinking floor in the living room, hoping I could rip something loose, dig my way out of the carpet, and escape, but the damaged flooring didn't budge an inch.

It sank several inches whenever people walked over it. Even Charlotte, the lightest of them all. The shitty sinking floor laughed in my face.

Floors can't usually laugh, but I've been trapped in someone's walls for five days, so I'm throwing my notion of what is or isn't possible out the window. Or, I would, if I could use one of the windows. I could push against them, go under, even over, but never through.

I don't think what I'm doing counts as living either. I don't sleep, or eat, or shit, or sweat. All the hammering against the floors and walls and ceilings didn't make me drip a single bead, which is great, because if I were trapped here *and* had to deal with body odor, I don't know what my life would come to.

Despite not being able to get out, there are areas where I can see in. These little 'windows' where windows shouldn't be, like one-way mirrors, except with paint and wood. There's one in every room, minimum, as many as four in the living room, giving me a great view of both the TV they watch, and them, as they watch the TV, if I scurry around to the other side.

Each bathroom has one to the side of the mirror, giving me a great profile view as George shaves, or Charlotte's daily pimple-assault ritual, or their profile as they fucked in the shower on Sunday morning, offering quiet moans in their porcelain church while the kid's still asleep. I don't treat it like porn. I treat it like *Animal Planet,* another afternoon special about some creature in the wild.

Now we see two mammals courting each other. This particular species, Homo Erectus, is known for arrogance and grandeur. They wear clothes and go to school and develop habits like playing the violin or criticizing art in order to fool themselves into thinking they aren't still the same savage, instinct-driven primates they evolved from, as demonstrated by their mating habits. In this instance, the male of this troop displays affection by groping the female's rear and waiting for further indication. If the female turns and smiles at him, or begins to remove her clothing, she will join the husband in the shower, where they apparently think running water will both muffle the sounds of their coupling and make them glisten like super models. They are seriously fucking wrong, but they're also fucking seriously, which is a rarity in domesticated humans, so good for them.

Five days. Five. Days. I've spent five days and five nights trapped in their walls, banging my fists, yelling for escape, and sure, it's my fault I wound up in there in the first place, but not escaping felt like *everyone's* fault. How don't they know they have a whole extra person living—or half-living, at least—in their walls? Can't they hear my footsteps, feel my breathing when I lean in close on those occasions they pass by my little windows?

My blows don't harm this house, but it doesn't harm me, either. No matter how many times I move a little too quickly or slam my fist into a surface a little too hard, I don't get scraped or bruised. I've smashed my head into seventeen different pipes—yes, I counted, because what else can I do here?—and no headaches or concussions. I haven't gotten a single splinter. The pain of smacking into something only lasts a second, then it fades to nothingness.

If I manage to get out, I'm going to pitch this idea to America's prison system. Sure, solitary is bad, but this lack of sensation is worse. To know that I'm *so close* so them, mere inches, in some cases, trapped behind a one-way pane of god-knows-what, able to scream and rage but never once be acknowledged, is maddening.

Day six made my situation a whole lot worse. Day six. God, how I wish I'd died on five so I didn't have to witness six. But that's not how life, or whatever happened to me, works.

Day six started like all the others. It was a Thursday. George squeezed Darleen's left breast while she was applying lipstick, causing her to jump and smear outside the lines, then playfully swat him. He left for work, hugging his daughter goodbye. Darleen blathered incessantly into a phone while washing dishes, telling a friend whose name I didn't catch that she was taking Charlotte to her Tuesday all-day child gymnastics play center thing. Darleen left at nine, according to the clock on the stove, and returned at ten-fifteen, according to the cable box. She returned with a man who definitely wasn't George and did things in their marital bed that made Sunday's shower sex look like a PBS after school special. They parted ways several hours later, having spoken maybe fifteen words to each other the whole time. Those words were mostly, "Take it off," "Yes!" and, "I didn't see that piercing before. Is it new?"

A few hours later, after Darleen had washed the sheets and picked her daughter up, who giggled happily about somersaults, George returned from work, looking pale and serious. He gave his daughter a kiss on the forehead, then entered the kitchen, where Darleen was loading the dishwasher, talking on the phone, oblivious to the water she was dripping on their cheap linoleum floor.

"Darleen." He entered the kitchen, face drawn, gaze downcast.

"Oh, you're home! Hi! Could you get me some paper towels from the basement?" she said without a glance in his direction.

He sighed and obliged, then, upon returning, set the roll on the counter, staring at her with heavy, unblinking eyes. When she finally caught on, she leaned away from the phone. "What's wrong?"

"We need to talk." Those four words slammed down on the kitchen like a mallet, the weight of their implication already enough to end their marriage. She gulped, said goodbye, and hung up the phone, setting it on the kitchen table, back to the sink.

"I'm sorry." Her eyes began to water.

"No, I… Wait, why are you sorry?" Confusion flickered on his face as if lit by a sudden bolt of lightning. His original train of thought was completely derailed.

"I… I didn't mean for it to happen, it's just… He's a single dad, and he's so great with kids. It's only been a few times, I swear."

A few times, for a woman as ritualistic as her, meant 'every week like clockwork since the first time,' but he didn't piece that together. Probably didn't want to. "What do you mean, a few times? What are you saying?" Then he finished that little puzzle, confusion turning to scorn. "You've been cheating on me?" These words came out hushed, as if Charlotte would understand what an affair was, and he didn't want to tarnish the way she thought about her mother.

Darleen nodded, trying not to break into sobs.

"For weeks?"

She nodded more, covering her face.

"Oh, this is just *perfect.*" Anger carved a swath of sarcasm through the otherwise lake-still surface of his suburban Dadhood. He kept his volume low, glancing toward the living room. "Here I was feeling guilty because Shannon kissed me over lunch today, and what, you've been having it off with some clown? What, did you go to the market for zucchinis, get confused, and screw the produce guy?"

"Hey, that is not how it happened!" Hands curled tight, her white knuckles shook. "I've seen him four, maybe five times!"

"Four, maybe five? Suddenly you can't remember how many times some other guy's been inside you? Or is it four, maybe five guys?"

"*One* guy, and I'm so busy watching after our daughter that, frankly, I don't remember exactly how many. It's not like you've been around to help!"

"I don't help? I don't help? I work! I work seventy hours a week, so we have a house, and clothes, and food—or do you not want those things? Would you maybe not fuck other guys if we lived under the Harrison Bridge, or slept in an abandoned shipping container eating beans out of a can?"

"Don't be an asshole about this!"

Neither of them seemed to give a damn what their daughter heard now, but she was obliviously watching some kids show. All I wanted to do was cover her ears and make sure she wouldn't hear. That wasn't really an option.

"Don't be an asshole? You cheated on me! Guess what: I'm allowed to be a little upset about that, Darleen. I'm allowed to be hurt. You don't get to betray me and then act surprised when I'm pissed off about it!"

She let out a long, heavy breath, air rushing through her nose so hard I expected an industrial steam-whistle screech to blast out, but that didn't happen. She just bit her lip and leaned against the counter, arms crossed.

"You're not going to say anything?" Anger provided very thin ice, tears already leaking through the cracks in his surface.

"What am I supposed to say?"

He looked away, staring a hole into the floor, as if he might escape into it. Or, at least, let me out. It was awkward enough having to hear them fuck, but now I'd have done pretty much anything to get away from them. "I don't know," he finally replied.

"Baby, you know I love you." She spoke softly, approaching him. "I made a mistake."

"Four or five mistakes."

She shut her eyes as if that'd soften the blow. "Okay. Yeah. Four or five. But he's just... a fling. It meant nothing."

"Ugh," he scowled. "Don't say that. You know how awful that sounds? It meant nothing? Don't tell me you threw away our marriage *for nothing*. It meant nothing means *I* mean nothing, it means us, this, all this," he waved at the house, at Charlotte, "meant nothing to you!"

"Hey, hey! Don't say that," she said, voice notably strained as she tried not to snap back at him. They didn't notice their daughter tilt her little head up and come bumbling toward the kitchen, crawling across the linoleum and under the table. "You know that's not true."

Darleen had gotten close enough to lay her hands on his arm, but he jerked them away as she pulled it toward her. "Don't touch me!" he said.

She took a few stumbling steps backward, then slipped in the water she'd spilled, upper body landing in the open dishwasher.

I saw what he didn't, at first. I screamed in the way he should've—in the way she couldn't anymore—heard my voice echo through the inside of the house, damned to never escape through to the outside world. Any call I made, a call for action, a call for help, died. I slammed my fists against the walls, yelling for that moron to do something, but he didn't notice that she'd been so distracted by her phone call that she'd loaded the knives point-up. Those points were now buried deep in the soft tissues of her neck. She struggled to get free, gagging, but the motion freed the blades, spewing blood through the wounds he hadn't yet noticed.

"Oh, now you're going to play the dramatic card just because you fell? Don't you try and earn fake sympathy points, you..."

Whatever name he was going to call her caught in his throat when he noticed the spreading pool of red in the basin of the dishwasher's door. His daughter sat quietly, not understanding the sight before her.

"Help her, jackass!" I screamed, but he didn't.

He stared, slack-jawed and eyes wide, for fifteen seconds, at least, before moving. He lifted her upper body, causing the knives to fall out of her, opening the wounds to let her bleed out. George reeled backward from the spray. I'm no mind reader, but I could see his thoughts on his face: a big fight; his prints on her clothes; her blood on his hands. All signs would point to domestic violence. At least, that's what he probably told himself.

He fled the room, knocking over the table in the process. The bang startled Charlotte, making her cry. If she hadn't figured out that there was something wrong with her parents by now, she sure as hell knew when her daddy dearest flew past her and right out the front door, without so much as a goodbye.

"Daddy?" She looked after him, talking so small and already scared of how strange her parents acted that I feared she might disappear entirely.

She stumbled over to the door and tried, oh god, how she tried to open the door, but couldn't. It made her tear up, made me feel worse, already on the verge of crying for her, when she stumbled back into the kitchen. She approached her mother's body, still whimpering, nudging her shoulder.

"Mommy, wake up." Her small voice disappeared in the horrible space of her empty kitchen, and she repeated "wake up" with more and more distress, until she realized her mother wasn't going to wake up. She shrieked, shrieked in the pitiful, helpless way only a child can when the world no longer makes sense. When they learn the hard way that parents aren't invincible, and they aren't always going to be there to help. When that child realizes *One of the only people I love is dead,* and *I'm going to die without her,* even if she didn't have the words to describe her anguish.

She fell back onto her rear and sobbed, screaming, wailing. She wet herself, and I looked away, trying to spare her dignity, because what else did she have left?

What did this kid—this orphan—have besides a little bit of privacy?

After a few minutes, her cries turned to whimpers. "Oh, kid," I groaned, looking down at her. "I'm so sorry."

Charlotte looked around, suddenly quiet. "H-hello?"

"Wait… can you hear me?"

She bumbled to her feet. "You're not mommy," she said, voice shaking, head turning. "You're not daddy."

"N-no, kid, I'm not. I'm not either." There were so many things I wanted to say: *How can you hear me? Can you open the crawlspace? Get me the fuck out of these walls!* But I had something more important to say. "It's gonna be alright. Maybe. In a while. I'm gonna help you though, okay?" She sniffled and nodded. "Your mommy's phone fell off the table. It's by the living room. Can you go get it?"

Charlotte followed my instruction, moving back around the table and finding her mom's brick of a cell phone. In time, I managed to get her to call 9-1-1, encouraging her to tell the operator the truth. She whimpered about how Daddy was gone and Mommy wasn't moving and everything was red. She gave her address, after I told her what it was.

After a pause, Charlotte added, "The person in the wall is being really nice to me."

A pause, then, "There's someone in the wall." Pause. "I don't know." Pause. "The person seems nice. I think they're my friend." Pause. "Hello?" she looked at the screen, but it was black.

Idiot Darleen must've killed the battery with all her chatter. Charlotte began to cry again.

"Hey, hey, it's okay, Charlotte."

It felt good to comfort her. Maybe, in some weird way, this is why I'd found myself trapped in the walls: So someone could be there for her.

"I'm here for you. Promise."

Twenty-five years later…

Chapter 1

arcy DuBois thought the call to see 417 Crows Drive nothing but a cheap prank. All the other calls had been pranks, after all, and after six months on the market with only bored teenagers ringing to see if *that* house came with a money-back guarantee in case of a haunting, she almost didn't bother answering the woman's message.

Her realtor training refused to let the message go unanswered, though, and the hunger in her heart to one day take over Glenfibbits and O'Halloran Realty meant forging ahead, even if the likelihood of selling 417 sat at next to nothing. She went through the typical motions, the ones every house deserved: lighting a candle so the place smelled of fresh cookies; vacuuming and dusting so it looked lived-in, and not chronically abandoned; making sure there were no unsightly, deal-breaking stains on the walls, rugs, hardwood, linoleum, ceramic, ceiling, and other myriad surfaces.

With all else said and done, she stood in the living room, pacing, eyes darting toward every corner to check for dust bunnies. Sitting would've been unprofessional, even if she could've comfortably sat, which ran a size tight several banana nut muffins ago. Everyone said to watch for cravings when giving up cigarettes, but she hadn't believed it. She did believe the scale. As with most women, some of that extra weight went to some aesthetically pleasing places, but her career ambitions hadn't allowed much of a love life recently, so there wasn't anyone around to admire her. None she *wanted* admiring her, at any rate.

To her complete shock, the lovely couple showed up. She couldn't believe the blue Tesla held her alleged buyers until the brake lights engaged, and the engine, against all odds, shut off. Marcy peered through the curtains as a woman just shy of thirty, not much younger than herself, hopped out of the driver's seat, while her husband left the passenger's, opening the back door. From there, he fiddled with a child's seat while the woman, presumably the mother, approached the house. Marcy opened the door and welcomed her inside.

"Hi, Ms. DuBois?" The woman, who up-close had a smile that shone brighter than the 2 PM sunlight all around them, extended her hand. In shaking it, she noticed smooth, cool skin. Hands that never performed labor, or even excessive handling—a well-educated white-collar type, probably looking for her first real home, the one she'd raise her child in. Marcy learned how to read people on the fly, and so far, her observations didn't bode well. A well-to-do woman wouldn't likely want to raise her child in this environment.

Snapping herself from her head, Marcy forced a smile and shook the hand. "Hi, yes, hello! I'm Marcy.

Please, by all means, just Marcy. You're Mrs. Burrows, right?"

"Yes, but just Charlotte, please." Charlotte beamed, not with the self-aggrandizement of some more upper-class socialite who loved hearing their own name, but sheer, genuine happiness at being recognized. Someone, perhaps, used to being overlooked?

The husband bumbled up with a sleeping daughter in his arms, her head laying across his shoulder, quietly snoring. He had a broad body, neither fat nor fit, but he probably could've been a fighter at some point. Big, calloused hands held his child, but didn't seem to have recent scrapes or blisters. A self-made man, who'd worked his way up in the world from oft-glorified humble origins—the kind that were only endearing to someone who'd never known the ensuing hardships. The child, maybe five, seemed small thanks to his muscular arms, but no, she ran on the tiny side. Pale, too. Had they kept her inside, as so many other parents did, where she'd be safe from allergens and kidnappers and sunburns, or did her petite size stem from an illness? Or, malnourishment? They didn't seem abusive, but she'd keep watch for signs, just in case.

"Ah, Marcy, this is my husband, Elijah, and daughter, Helena."

"Hi there. I'd shake your hands, but..." He nodded to his kid. His lips smiled, but his eyes and voice didn't. Slow to trust. Another bad sign. Between him having a guard up and Little Miss Sunshine wanting the perfect play palace for her princess, this sale, the first hint of one in almost half a year, had likely gone belly-up before they walked in the door.

Still, she considered herself a professional, even if some of those at her office disagreed. The older types thought that scented candles and pastel ornamentation were cheap tricks, but they derived from proven scientific inquiry. Well, semi-scientific, at least. Bright colors and sweet smells trick the brain into feeling comfortable and safe, like it's already home.

As an added benefit, the cookie smell might get the daughter on board. If Helena wanted to stay, she might be the extra nudge necessary to get her parents to close.

At least, they'd be ready until she reached the 'disclosure' point. Houses that come with 'gruesome death' on the record do not sell well, no matter how many bathrooms they have. There's no such thing as a new homeowner, just the newest. Or, as some might say, the last.

They walked further into the house, and Marcy let them take in the environment she'd worked so hard to maintain. The walls let out a groan, creaking in that odd way she only ever heard here. Charlotte turned her head toward the sound with a look of vacant amazement. Marcy spoke up, mentioning that the building was still settling from recent renovations, but only Elijah looked her way. She didn't believe that, anyway.

Once Charlotte's spell had been broken, Marcy tried again. "So are you two from the area, or are you looking to move down this way?" She'd practiced all sorts of pitches, lines, and deals to cater to different types of couples, as any good realtor should.

"I… guess you'd say I'm from the area. My husband isn't." She smiled at her dearly beloved. "He runs a business nearby, and this is closer to his office than our apartment. I work from home, so distance isn't an issue."

Marcy smiled at Helena. "With this little one, I imagine you want space for her to grow up and run around, huh?" They grinned, clearly proud parents. "How old is she, if she doesn't mind my asking?" The realtor gave a cheesy, friendly smile, forcing the joke.

Snorting back a laugh, Charlotte waved her off. "Oh, I don't think people mind being asked their age until they hit their mid-twenties. That's about when growing up stops being cool. No more thrill of adulthood, no first drinks and late-night clubs, just bills. Not that I was the clubbing type. Had our daughter when I was twenty-three, and she's five now, at the risk of dating myself."

Another practiced smile from Marcy. "If it's any consolation, I'm a few months older than you, so you've got that going."

Charlotte shrugged, looking over at her husband with the bright goo-goo eyes of a newlywed couple—or someone who thinks love is all she can rely on, based on the little twist of sorrow in the creases of her face. "I don't worry much about getting old these days. I'd rather live well than for a long time." He looked back with the same happy-sad expression.

Perfect: cheesy co-dependent puppy love, the bloom of youth tempered by hardship. That factor, she could work with, and did, showing them everything. The kitchen came equipped with a vented range hood, brand-new refrigerator (courtesy of the last occupants), and nearly forty feet of counterspace. From there, they looked out through a sliding glass door at the spacious, fenced-in backyard, then stepped back in to look at the pantry. Creaks followed them all the while, like an invisible fifth presence. Charlotte kept looking toward the sounds but would snap her attention back moments later.

The pantry had a small door at the bottom that would've once led to a crawlspace. The building went through several renovations throughout the past two decades, sealing it over in the process. Another door in the kitchen led to the basement, where the water filter, boiler, and all other house guts boasted recent inspection stickers. Its ceiling sat high enough overhead where they didn't have to worry about bumping pipes or vents.

Marcy also pointed out where the crawlspace ran, clearly marked off by a difference in the ceiling boards, and a cubby space behind a brick wall opposite the stairs, where the foundation supports rested.

At no point did her observation skills tell her the one fact that determined make-or-break status before she'd even begun talking. She didn't notice it when pointing out the two full baths, or the half-bath, or the three bedrooms. Marcy's attention divested itself in explaining the various storage spaces of the house, so much so that she paid no mind to the fact that Charlotte knew, off-hand, that the attic could only be accessed through a trapdoor in the closet of one of the guest rooms, as that was the one element no renovation had touched.

"Now that we've gone through the tour, I do have to mention…" Marcy sighed, trying to convey mild annoyance rather than fear or despair. "This house has a history."

"I know." Charlotte nodded, looking at her husband. The floor groaned beneath them, as if protesting the new line of conversation. "We've talked about it."

Great. Of course they knew. Those 'look up if anyone's died here' sites were usually a scam, but when legitimate news sources wrote up articles, it got difficult to keep things quiet. Part of why 417 never got calls.

"Yes, well, I understand it can be intimidating, a house with, you know… death on the registry." Marcy hated this part. The inevitable, "Sorry, you're great, but maybe we'll look somewhere else."

"We're fine with that. We'll take it."

"You see, if… I'm sorry, come again?" Marcy tilted her head, as if she'd hear the expected response by bringing her ear closer to Charlotte's mouth. There's no way she actually said she was fine with what she'd read.

"Every house has a history. This is the perfect location, it has room for Helena, room for guests… Besides, living here knowing that it happened can't be worse than watching it happen." She looked toward the kitchen as her husband freed a hand to rub her back.

They weren't connecting. Marcy didn't want to risk the sale, but still had to say something. "Certainly, yes, but I'd be remiss if I didn't inform you—"

"Let me stop you, because frankly, I don't want to relive it." Charlotte held up a hand to cut her off, still trying damn hard to be polite about being rude. With a heavy sigh and the distant, far-off tone of a person who wasn't really present, she looked up toward the kitchen. "I was here when… you know. I used to live here. Mom died… right over there." She pointed to the dishwasher, shiny and gray as a freshly-washed blade, still visible from their spot in the living room.

Marcy blanched, a hand rising to her throat, as if to catch the breath that had been knocked free of her body. She didn't know what to say. Nothing in her training covered this, and she'd never experienced a child coming back to buy her parent's home after their death. She'd sold houses left in wills when the child didn't want it, but this? All unknown territory.

"I'm… so sorry." It barely counted as a response, but at least Marcy hadn't let this news sink into the silence.

"Don't be. It happened a long time ago." Charlotte snapped back to reality, then chuckled. "I… probably could've told you sooner. Nearly a quarter century later and it's still hard to talk about. Point is, I know what happened here. I'm okay with that. I waive everything pertaining to the death disclosure. I just… I look around and feel like I'm home."

Elijah cast a sidelong glance at his wife, wary, but with a hint of a grin suggesting he supported her. Maybe this place, despite its history, would work for the happy couple.

Helena stirred against her father's shoulder, sniffing the air. "Cookies?" Her tiny voice all but mumbled it, and her parents laughed, Elijah rubbing her back to lull her back to sleep. Marcy didn't pry, but a sudden glassiness in Charlotte's eyes told her the child wasn't well after all. If the woman hadn't teared up at remembering her own mother's death, then whatever this family had faced, or still faced, must have been unspeakable.

She turned away to avoid tearing up, too. The adult world seemed so full of death and suffering, between increasing drug use, existing wars, impending wars, hurricanes, and resurging illnesses. Their chaos shouldn't have to leak over to the children.

Marcy, as a professional, could've objected to them waiving the death disclosure section, or said more, or done her diligence and at least made her sign a real waiver, but as a person, she couldn't bear to put Charlotte through more pain. She could call another time, she reasoned. Talk to Elijah, tell him the details of the dozens of people who'd died there in the past twenty-five years to make sure he's aware. Charlotte might've witnessed one, but the happy couple should know about all of them. People called that house cursed for a reason.

Yes, that made sense, didn't it? Tell them, tell one of them, for the sake of their marriage. She believed in love, and that love requires honesty. If Charlotte had trouble talking about this, or simply didn't want to know, he ought to know everything, from one source or another.

There remained paperwork to fill out, red tape, legalese, payments, but as far as she cared, they were set. They took the remaining time of the 'tour' to check over everything and put it in writing. A few signatures here, an exchange of information, and to Marcy's absolute surprise, it sold. 'That House,' no longer on the market, all thanks to her. Let the bastards say she's not a realtor now.

She grinned to herself, packing the papers up. Today demanded celebration. She'd buy a pack on the way home, the good smokes, no light crap, and walk into the office smoking. They didn't like that, she'd puff right in their faces, laugh like hell if they told her she couldn't.

Really, she knew luck made the sale. Luck, nostalgia, and timing. If any other person had wanted to see 417, they probably would've left, like any other person. But still, the first serious call about 'That House,' and she closed the sale that same day?

No way she wasn't celebrating.

Marcy waved goodbye as she stepped outside, shutting the door behind her. They had the keys. She no longer had to concern herself with 417 Crows Drive. 'That House' belonged to the couple now, and among all the excitement, her self-imposed duty to call Elijah later on fled her mind, entirely forgotten.

Chapter 2

harlotte took a slow breath, gazing around her new home in awe. Well, she supposed it was her old home, made new again by time and unfamiliarity. After all, she'd been there before.

She was afraid to inhale too sharply for fear of waking up. Dreaming could be the only real explanation here. She'd fallen asleep at some point, maybe on the couch, during the latest episode of *Channel Zero's* second season. Elijah probably saw her face, serene, nose twitching in response to some pseudo-reality that only existed in her head and decided not to disturb her. He always did that—let her sleep whenever and wherever she conked out.

"You run yourself ragged!" He'd said, jokingly, only two weeks earlier. "You make your own schedule, so why push yourself to stay up all night, wake up early, meet these insane deadlines?"

Of course, that only held half the truth—her clients had deadline expectations too—but her work ethic did lead to a lot of spontaneous naps. Charlotte pinched herself. Dug her nails into the soft underside of her left wrist. Apparently awake, she told herself she wasn't dreaming, still not fully able to believe it.

"So, we're homeowners now," Elijah said, putting Helena down on the couch, where she instinctively curled around a throw pillow, hugging it tight. "Excited? I know I am, and considering what this house meant to you…"

"I think so. Still can't fully wrap my head around it. To think we got it so quickly, and for such a great price!" She smiled, big and wide, but as the curve slowly inverted, she looked back at the kitchen, then up toward the bedrooms, as if peering through the floors with x-ray vision. Charlotte paced a little, eyes darting back and forth, scanning the scatter of her thoughts, before she bit her lip and straightened up. "You don't think it's a crazy idea, do you? Why I wanted this place?"

"Not at all, sweetheart, no, not at all." He walked over and wrapped his arms around her, a hug he hoped would convey warmth and security, to pull her back out of her own head. At a few inches taller than her, he always worried a hug would feel confining, or like he dwarfed her in some way. "You have every reason to want to be here. Your reasoning makes sense, and I fully support this move." Then, with a kiss to her forehead, he added, "I wouldn't have moved here if it didn't."

She nestled in against his chest, but her heart wasn't in it. He could tell. He knew her well enough by now to know when her body ran on autopilot, the rest of her occupied by other matters. There were *always* other matters, real or imaginary, but he didn't mind. They hadn't married to spend every waking second in rapt attention to one another. If each didn't give the other space to breathe, they'd both suffocate. Especially now, when he spent half his time making sure she wouldn't find one of James's socks tucked off in the corner of a duffle bag, or one of his drawings floating around in their packed-up belongings. Remembering him mattered, but she needed preparation. Time. A warning. Too sudden, and he worried she'd have a break down.

"Maybe we picked a bad time. Do you think? I mean, Helena only got the all-clear the other day, and she'll need monitoring, a stable environment, certain protections, safeguards…" Her words trailed off into a mumble. Though he couldn't hear her, he knew what she said, what ran through her mind. The doctors had given all sorts of recommendations—some conflicting—and neither of them wanted to see her back in the hospital.

Elijah did his absolute best to reassure her, not that he felt confident, either. Even if every recommendation got followed to the last letter, barring those that canceled each other out ("Make sure she exercises to build her strength up again." "Make sure she gets plenty of rest, no exertion, no running around." Among others.) there remained a chance of her developing more issues.

"Besides, I think this is the best time." Now Elijah spoke as much to assure himself as his wife. "This is a controlled environment. Living in an apartment building, there's no telling what pathogens get left in the rugs, sneak into the vents, get breathed out as you pass people by in the halls, and we're not even talking pests. Could you imagine how much it would suck to bring her back from the hospital, only to learn we have rats and bedbugs?"

She laughed and slapped at his chest. They'd lived in a good building, no such problems, not even remotely. The landlord and building manager had both been extremely cautious about such matters, just as they'd been understanding when, after Helena and James first got sick, they'd forgotten to pay rent.

Turning to her sleeping child, Charlotte fought the urge to cry. Helena already missed her brother enough. Seeing Mommy cry wouldn't ease her pain.

"Plus, I guess it'll be good to, you know, not be there anymore. Too many memories. I mean, she's still a kid, but... even young, a brother's a brother." They'd had a lot of not-talks about this. Sitting in silence, mourning him together, thinking the same thoughts, unable to speak them aloud. Helena, for the most part, had been too ill to really sink into that sadness.

Each time she woke up enough to be lucid, she'd ask, "Where's James?" Then they'd remind her he'd gone to another place, that he couldn't come home, and she'd cry, just a little. A lethargic rolling-down-the-face of tears she barely had the energy to produce. Helena would fall back asleep after a bit, already exhausted by waking up, further drained by the news.

Then she'd wake up, after a while, and ask about him again.

Every single time.

Elijah stiffened against Charlotte, struggling with his own emotions. Neither of them wanted their new life to be about living in pain, but they couldn't just forget about their child. Still, where does the line get drawn? At what point does moving on cease to be disrespectful?

Tory, one of Elijah's sisters, a clinical psychologist, reminded them that the DSM-V states the grieving period lasts two weeks, at which point it becomes clinical depression, and they should seek counseling, perhaps pharmaceutical intervention. She'd already been a somewhat estranged family member. Now, they didn't speak at all. Then again, it's hard to call someone up for a Sunday afternoon chat over coffee after getting thrown out of a funeral.

On the couch, Helena rolled over, almost falling off the couch, but her father disentangled himself to race over, catching her before that happened. A broken bone would be insult to injury, at this point. They didn't need to go racing back to the doctors for some new issue. Not when still dealing with her symptoms and complications.

Of course, Charlotte didn't tell him the entire reason for wanting to move back 'home.' Despite loving her adoptive parents, and growing up in their house, a little piece of her past haunted her since the day her mother died: the voice she'd heard. The one that guided her on how to call emergency services, the one that echoed in her ears every time she went to dial because she didn't know her numbers, and the voice wanted to make sure someone could help her. The presence in the house that had seemed to echo from everywhere at once.

When she first entered the house again, she'd heard creaking that could've been the floorboards, or the house settling. Some of the floors had clearly undergone recent renovation anyway, but Marcy and Elijah had given no indication to hearing it. Hair raised on her neck, the feeling of eyes on her coming from all sides. She couldn't quite put her finger on why, but she could swear it still lingered, this being, spirit, whatever it called itself, and that it watched from within the walls.

She heard groans from all sides, scrapes and scuffles, like someone moving around in there. Occasionally, something would bump underfoot, the sound of a person hitting their head on a beam or knocking on the underside of the living room. Her wardrobe flickered briefly through her mind. If it really did live here, in the walls and floors, she'd never be able to wear a skirt again. Charlotte only owned a few anyway, though, so that didn't matter to her. At least, it didn't matter as much as figuring out what had spoken to her all those years ago.

She'd talked about it at the time, but the orphanage staff just passed her off to a child psychologist, who rationalized it away, telling her, pointedly, that she hadn't heard anything, and her scared brain made her think that after the fact, so everything made sense. *Do you understand now, sweetie? You didn't hear anything.* The shrink smiled, sweet as cyanide, her teeth yellow with a hint of smeared red lipstick, a color combo that led her to think a psychologist is just someone with a head full of piss and blood. At four, she hadn't used those exact words, but the idea lasted, and Tory hadn't changed her opinion.

Stepping away from Elijah, Charlotte figured, if she were going to reconnect with her roots, and whatever might be living here, she ought to start in the kitchen. That's where everything began, after all. Her feet clacked over the wood, hand drifting lazily onto a cheap round table that they'd likely throw away. The realtor said they could keep the furniture, likely part of sweetening the sale of a 'difficult' house, but these staging items weren't exactly high quality.

Creaks and groans followed her, settling near the doors to the backyard. Her skin tingled as if she were being watched from that same direction. Whispering so Elijah wouldn't hear—she couldn't tell him about it until she was absolutely sure—she whispered, "Hello?"

You're back.

The reply came immediately, a little colder than she remembered as a kid, but just as real as it had been when Marcy showed her around, the ice water words dripping in her ears and creeping slowly into her brain. It gave her chills, her heart racing.

Charlotte smiled all the same.

"Yeah. I'm here."

Welcome home.

Chapter 3

Many consider moving to be one of the most stressful events a person can go through, but for Charlotte, everything sailed by on a cloud. If any problems arose, they solved themselves long before she became aware of them. Her husband, too, seemed unperturbed, his normal need to oversee and micromanage every aspect of a major event quelled by the fact that nothing needed managing.

The movers arrived with what little they'd needed moved an hour early. Every appliance ran without a hitch. The fridge stayed cold, not like the one from her starter apartment, which died within hours of her moving in. Clothes got wet in the washer and dry in the dryer without her having to crank everything to the highest setting to get a semblance of their original functions. When they unpacked the boxes and checked out their microwave and toaster against those that came with the house, she found the 'show' set far better than the set they'd brought. Elijah didn't love the fact that the toaster beeped to announce having completed toasting, but he liked that it wasn't a several-years-old model.

Nearly everything about this house, she found, was to her liking. Fresh, new carpeting spanned from wall to wall, free from the dust and dirt of previous owners. All the bedrooms had bright, cheery paint colors, the master bearing a dusky orange, glowing like warm earth settling in for the night. There were two guest bedrooms, and Helena chose the one with a whitish-green color, because it felt like being outside. Elijah and Charlotte shared a look—they both wished they could let her outside more, but for the past thirteen months, that simply hadn't been an option. Maybe now, with a backyard, some time, and a doctor's recommendation, that would change. Hopefully, at least. She had to stay hopeful.

The kitchen tiles had been replaced recently, as had the dishwasher, so if her mother's blood had stained anything, those things were no longer here as macabre reminders of why she wanted to move back in the first place. The only other reminder creaked through the walls, watching, occasionally whispering, and in moments of privacy, when Elijah watched over Helena, or if he stepped out and their daughter napped, Charlotte whispered back. She never spoke at a regular volume, though. She didn't like diving straight into pools, literally or otherwise, and this water sent excited chills through her.

Charlotte came to swim but needed to adjust to the temperature first.

How old is she?

"Five," Charlotte whispered, peeking in at her daughter, who sat at a tea party table, pretending her toys came for an afternoon get together. She poured tea, walking slowly, being careful when most children wouldn't have even known what careful was. One day, her illness would be a blip in her life's memory, but until then, Charlotte waited. Unlike most mothers, she couldn't wait to see her daughter forget caution altogether.

Five. You were… Three, I believe, when you left?

"Yeah. Not that I had a choice in leaving, though." She walked downstairs, where she could whisper without the possibility of bothering her daughter. Given that it was 2 o'clock on a Wednesday afternoon, Elijah had gone off to work hours ago, and wouldn't be back for a while yet.

Faint creaks and groans followed her, footsteps taking long, steady strides. Charlotte had no idea what the being in the wall might look like. Sometimes, the sounds seemed pretty normal, matching pace with her gait; at others, she'd hear noises so spaced apart, she had to believe its arms and legs were mile-long snakes coiled up in circles, extending to suit its needs.

It couldn't be a ghost, though. Sure, it had been in the walls for twenty-five years now—at least—and apparently didn't need to eat, drink, or relieve itself. Its voice came as a breathy whisper in the back of her mind, wind through trees dying in October's first deep chill, neither male nor female, rather than something she heard with her ears. All this *might* have suggested a ghost, if not for the sounds. It walked, climbed, slithered in the floors, never moving into an actual room, never joining them at the dinner table, but always physical. She could hear it move, feel it watch her from nearby. Yet, her intuition told her that breaching the walls wouldn't set it free. That the walls housing Charlotte weren't the walls housing the presence. Not exactly.

"I don't think I ever got to thank you." Charlotte turned her eyes to the closest approximation she could manage of where it seemed to be. Guessing its location meant relying on where the creaks stopped, and which parts of her skin pricked up with the sense of being stared at from the shadows. "Young as I was, I don't think I would've known what to do. I wouldn't have," she scoffed. "No child would. So… thank you, for helping me. You might've saved my life that day."

Seems so long ago, but I remember you didn't hear me until… after. I'd been trying to get someone's attention. Then, I spoke, and you responded. You were the first, but not the last.

"Other people have heard you, too?" Her heart gave a hard thump, a punch to her ribcage, trying to get her attention. A surprise surge of jealousy heated her veins. Adults cling to the little private memories from their childhoods, the fleeting moments where stars align, and they feel something beyond themselves before losing that cosmic connection to the humdrum of nine-to-fives and taxes. That little private memory of her talking to the person in the walls was no longer hers. It stung enough to bring old tears to her eyes.

Yes, others have. But you will always have been first. You hearing me made me realize I could, in fact, be heard. You gave me hope. So don't cry.

Charlotte wiped hastily at her eyes. "Sorry." Her whisper felt ineffective, sheepish. She laughed at herself, if only to break the ensuing silence. "I just… it's one of the reasons I moved back here. I wanted to… get to know you. Figure you out. See if you were still here."

Well, I am. Obviously. Would you have wanted to live here if I wasn't? I wonder what you would've done, had you spoken to these walls, and only received silence in reply.

She shrugged. "No idea. It's a beautiful house, with enough bedrooms to… Well, if we thought of having more kids. That might be a little ways off, but it's close to Elijah's office, has a backyard, a good school system nearby. It's hard to pass up a home like this, especially since the realtor let it go for a great price. I guess death in the house will do that, huh?" Charlotte offered a weak smile at her surroundings.

Accidents happen.

Yeah, accidents do happen, but her life had been shaped by what others said about her mother's death. She didn't remember much: arguing, a thump from the dishwasher, Daddy running away, the voice talking in her head. A few vague flashes from before that day painted her dad as an overall okay guy, but she'd been too young to form any stable, clear memories.

"Everyone says it had been domestic violence. Manslaughter, but still. The orphanages, my foster parents, no one ever wanted to talk about it, just said it was good I didn't live with him. In high school, I looked at some old newspapers at the library. The papers all suggested he killed her. Maybe by accident, but everyone called my biological dad a murderer. He did run off. No one's seen him since. …I don't suppose you… remember. Do you?"

Her throat kept catching her voice, tangling it up in vines of mucus and pent-up emotion. Even the therapist she saw in middle school didn't want to talk about this. She and Elijah had, of course, but Charlotte didn't want to burden him with her own ancient history. The presence, though, the person in the walls, who'd been there when it happened, might have more to say.

Like I said: accidents happen. They argued. She put her hand on his arm, tried to console him, and he jerked back. She slipped on spilled water. I'll spare you the gory details, but... it wasn't his fault. Not directly. I'm sure he never meant to hurt her. I imagine he left to avoid getting arrested. I don't know why he left you behind.

The words faded into nothingness, because that's what the being had offered her: nothingness. There'd been no real reason for her father to abandon her, no home invasion gone awry, no psychotic episode, no mafia hit that sent him running so the goons wouldn't come after his daughter to hurt him, none of the wild lies she'd told herself to give it all meaning. If this presence told the truth, then reality was far worse than what the news had reported, or what the police assumed. In reality, she'd slipped, fallen, and died. A life snuffed out in a second because of a puddle on linoleum, the course of her own life irreparably altered by a man who so greatly feared being accused of a crime that he'd leave his own child to die.

"That's... bullshit. That's really the story? That my mom was a klutz, and my dad a coward? I got trapped by a stupid spring-latch bolt and would've starved to death while she rotted in the next room, all because of a puddle?" Her eyes watered, this time with new pain. Anger flared in her stomach, body boiling with fresh acid, ready to burn someone, but her anger had no target.

It's clearly not what you wanted to hear. But, what would you have preferred? I can't think of a story I could've told, of any lie I might've concocted, that would ease your pain. The reality is terrible, no matter the lens you look through.

"I just thought there might've been a bigger reason. Not even a 'grand scheme of things' interpretation, but an important motivation, some kind of catalyst. Hell, I'd have taken brutal murder over a stupid accident." Charlotte paced through the kitchen, acutely aware that no footsteps sounded to pace alongside her, but with no one to look at and a lot of excess energy now, she couldn't sit still.

Your life is yours. Regret it, resent it, or move past it. You're here now, with a child of your own. Isn't that the important part? The present, rather than the past?

Her pacing slowed, but didn't stop, anger ebbing out, leaving emptiness behind. "The present is inexorably shaped by the past. Things are as they are because of what was, and..." She looked up at the ceiling, as if peering through to Helena. "I wouldn't ever want to live a life without my daughter. But still, how might my life have been different?" She didn't give voice to the dagger of a thought that pierced her heart: Would my son be alive, if I'd had my biological parents to warn me of what I might pass on?

Different is rarely better. All the years I've been in this house, watching, I've seen the occupants suffer. Every single one of them had pain. Something to complain about. Every single one of them tried to cure that pain, and simply traded one agony for another. You might have been better off in some respects, but far worse in others.

Charlotte stopped, leaning back against the stove. "Helena had a brother. James. They both got sick, but he didn't make it. A hereditary disease that I passed on. If my parents had been alive to warn me..."

Ah. I see. Death sent you away, and death brought you back.

She wanted to look away, annoyed at the suggestion that her life hadn't changed, simply come full circle, a wheel turning back to the same tired, rusty spoke, but she didn't know where to turn. James's death couldn't be that pointless. She would've found her way back here in time. No, his death wouldn't be the fuel for some reductionist argument that he had to die for her to come home.

"Maybe." It would be as close as she could come to saying *Fuck off,* because she didn't want to piss it off—both because she'd waited so long to talk to it again, and she didn't know what it could do. Instead, she asked for some time alone, stating that she wanted a little time alone, which was true enough.

The presence granted her request, ending the conversation. It waited twenty-five years for her return, though, and didn't feel inclined to simply sit around. There were other ideas, avenues, realms of possibility to attend to. Reaching up, it clambered through the walls, silently, as it had learned to move long ago. The house no longer creaked or groaned unless it wanted it to, and right now, it had no interest in Charlotte knowing where it went.

Climbing up to the guest room, it found the daughter sitting at a cheap plastic table, pouring imaginary tea for imaginary friends, seats occupied by dolls so new they still had price tags. A mountain of similar toys sat stacked in the corner, the dresser tops clogged by knickknacks and trinkets, her few shelves adorned with gifts. Judging by the dust, she hadn't gotten to, or hadn't bothered to, play with many of them.

Hello, little one.

Helena's head perked up. She looked around, eyes eventually settling on where she thought the voice originated. Even though it echoed in her head, she had a feeling it came from the wall across from her bed. That didn't seem right, but she talked back anyway.

"Hello. ...Who are you?"

Chapter 4

Elijah had to admit, the move went smoothly, and everyone settled into the house like they'd lived here all along. Charlotte, in particular, seemed at ease. At peace, even. She'd always been on the jumpier side, distrusting. One of the reasons she never held a real job for long, why she worked from home instead. Here, none of that. Even after James, she seemed relaxed.

Every now and again, the house would groan in a weird way, but at nearly eighty years old, any building would get a little loud. A dwelling that went through several renovations certainly came with an excuse for the occasional settling sounds.

They hadn't been to any doctor since about a week prior to the move. The radiologist, the oncologist, the therapists, none of them. A fresh start, that's what this was, a chance to rebuild, make a brand-new life in the absence of a young one. He didn't like the idea of erasing his son, but maybe moving on means no longer thinking about someone, filling the silence of their life with the sounds of someone else's.

Helena needed their attention, at any rate. He told himself that her health was his top priority, because if anything happened, Charlotte wouldn't survive losing her, too. He only held this belief to avoid admitting he wouldn't make it, either. Paul, his father, raised him to be a family man, and a family man with no family isn't anyone at all.

Yes, this would be their new home, their homestead, even. Charlotte could rebuild herself, throw any extra energy into her work, just as he had. Ostensibly, it'd been easy to claim he went to work more to afford the extra bills. Insurance only covered so much, after all. But no, no, he had to be strong for her, so when he couldn't stand how quiet their apartment got, or how loud the hospital was, he went to work. He made plans, oversaw extra projects, went to their construction sites to meet with contractors, foremen, forewomen, whoever. Doing so kept his mind occupied, and his eyes dry. Besides, they wound up taking on so many additional projects over the past few months, from the skyscraper in Durham to the restorations on the Cavanaugh estate in Ivy's Path, that they practically supplied half the new construction in Massachusetts, or so he liked to joke. They needed his expert eyes whenever he could spare them.

Now, at their new home, he, too, found the silence welcoming. It didn't feel lonely, like the apartment had. When Charlotte took Helena out, he could sit on the couch, a coffee or beer in hand, depending on the time, and enjoy the space. This place listened—not like an apartment building, where there's always a nosy neighbor to eavesdrop on your private conversations, but more like a church. A presence filling every room that seems to cloak you in reassurance, hearing every word, no matter how quiet the whisper.

The third Saturday after they moved in, Helena wanted to accompany Charlotte to the grocery store. Her lab work came back with an all-clear from the doctor to do minor exertion—like walking around the store—so they agreed their daughter could handle it, leaving him to do Sudoku at the kitchen table.

"If I put a nine here… no, wait, shit. I mean, darn." He covered his mouth, then remembered no one could hear him. "I mean shit, actually. Yeah. Shouldn't have done this in pen." Shaking his head, he rose from the chair and headed upstairs to Charlotte's office. He didn't have much work to do outside the offices, so he used a laptop for the occasional meander around the internet, leaving the desktop system and home office set-up to his wife. What use did he have for that space, or the equipment?

He did, however, want to steal a piece of printer paper so he could copy down the original puzzle and try again. It'd bother him if he just walked away from it because he forgot to grab a pencil first, so he walked up to the second floor. He gave a lot of credit to whoever oversaw the remodel, because the stairs led directly into the center, with the 'hallway' wrapping around it, like a catwalk in an esteemed mansion, from which the wealthy owner could look down at the guests filling his grand foyer and give speeches. The second floor didn't offer a view to the first, but it still made Elijah feel like a king, in some ways, to walk its interesting design.

Charlotte's office looked the way one would expect an office to look, but he couldn't help adore the little touches that made it *her* office. Sure, it had a few bookshelves lined with novels, marketing handbooks, and other manuals, and yes, a desktop computer sat quietly beneath a large wooden desk, where his wife would keep watch, working with the unrelenting focus of the Queen's Guard. That didn't stop her from having The Deadly Dictionaries, all seven, piled up next to the monitor. She never used them but loved the novelty. Gargoyles perched on almost every other shelf, one of which housed collected volumes of *Deadpool,* who she favored over all other comic figures because he can talk to the narrative boxes.

On their third date, they'd stumbled into a discussion of comic books after making the mistake of seeing *X-Men: The Last Stand,* a wildly misleading title considering there'd been another four or so movies and several shows featuring those characters since its release. Seeing *Logan* on TV brought that age-old discussion back around again. "There's something so… endearing about it, you know? I love the fact that he talks to this voice. He knows it's there, and it's real! People call him insane—even he thinks he's insane, and, well, he kind of is—but as the reader, we understand that the narrator is as real a presence, as important a character, as any other. The narrator is usually just a character to the reader, but for Wade, it's a thinking, engaging being he can interact with. Isn't that kind of great?"

Charlotte had been asleep upstairs since 8:30, and he had to be up at 5 for an early start. A glance at the blinking 10:37 on their cable box told him all he needed to know about whether he wanted to really talk about this. "It's interesting, I give you that much, but you're the fiction-type here, not me."

He liked reading, too, but preferred memoir. Something about having that private window into someone's life, where you could peer into their past without them knowing you were there, felt empowering. It gave him insight to how other people think. Of course, he only got the insight the authors wanted to give, and only saw the events they decided to write about, but still, he enjoyed it.

On his way out of his wife's office, pristine white paper held gently in one of his calloused hands, he saw Helena's door ajar. The other doors all sat open. One of Charlotte's little quirks. She hated closed doors. The doors leading outside were obvious exceptions, but bedroom, bathroom, closet, even the basement, sat wide open. A shut door in their house seemed about as natural as a quarterback playing the Super Bowl in a frilly pink dress.

Circling the upstairs, he crossed to Helena's room and nudged the door open, not sure what he expected. At five, almost six, she still had years to go before any rebellious teenager stage where she might be inclined to hide something or keep secrets. At five, what secrets could she even have? There might be things she kept from peers, but her parents, no, she couldn't get up to any funny business without their knowing. At her absolute worst, what little she tried to hide usually didn't matter much, in the grand scheme. A wet bed. A broken cup she tried to get from the cabinet herself. A rogue sneeze that meant Mr. Teddy had to go through the wash again.

After a few months in the hospital, between illness and muscle weakness, she didn't much have the strength to hide things these days. Just going to the store with Charlotte had been good. No, it was *great* that she went, not just because she had the strength to go, but she believed in herself enough to ask.

Trying not to let his eyes water at this thought, he looked around his daughter's room. Stuffed animals lined a few shelves, but she had far less than she could've. When James died, they offered her his toys, but she said no—donate them. So they did.

Her bed, nicely made, with Mommy's help, of course. More accurately, Mommy made it, and Charlotte smoothed the covers after. Two pillows, two throw pillows, Mr. Teddy perched in the center, resting. A tiny table, kid sized, for tea parties.

One empty chair.

Elijah furrowed his brow, looking at this void where a toy should've sat. Helena always served a full house, refused to leave a single seat vacant, even if that meant having Daddy perch himself in the way-too-small-for-him seat, legs tucked under him, so he didn't topple helplessly forward, or hit himself in the jaw with his knees.

The other chairs all had dolls or stuffed creatures occupying them, ready to drink illusionary tea at a moment's notice. They angled slightly, as if facing this empty seat, and a cursory glance told him the honored guest hadn't simply fallen or been misplaced. It didn't lay on the floor, hadn't been stashed under the bed, and she didn't have the height to reach the shelves. Yet, he remembered about their first days here, and how they'd set up her room, he and Charlotte working hard while Helena played Mr. Daddy, directing them to lift with their back, and warning that the floor was cement. Helena made sure every seat sat occupied.

This might not have been too odd, except the place setting vanished, too. No cup, no saucer, no plate, no utensils. Just a picture sitting where such items would've rested. From his view, it sat upside down, but it wasn't a complicated drawing. Three people, drawn in with pencil, the pencil drawn over with crayon, holding hands in front of their house, complete with the roof, chimney, and sidewalk-mounted mailbox.

His stomach turned a bit as he looked at the way she drew the house, and Elijah walked around the table to get a better angle. Even as the door opened and shut downstairs, he didn't slow, or hasten, or turn away, but knelt down on the rug, picking up the picture.

The house didn't have upper story windows. Not the way she drew it. No, Helena drew eyes instead. Two big, dark, bloodshot eyes sunk into the face of the house, pinprick pupils glaring at him from irises gray as death. The way the three figures in front held hands gave the appearance of a grin, their black stick arms curling up in a way that made his blood run cold.

"Daddy?" Helena said from the doorway, snapping him out of his trance. She rubbed at her face sleepily, eyes drooping, but her skin flushed and colorful. Just tired. Not ill, not passing out. He let out a relieved sigh. "What are you doing?"

"I… wanted to look at this pretty picture you drew of us." He held it to face her, as if she hadn't seen if before. "You're such a talented artist!" Like every parent, his duties included all the supportive, ego-boosting compliments he could muster, but not this time. The eyes were a little too real for a child her age. This was real talent, and really worrisome. "But can I ask you something, sweetie?"

She nodded, bumbling over to nuzzle her head against his side, taking a seat on his knee. He wrapped his arm around her, keeping her supported as her back slackened. Kids had toppled from more secure heights easily enough without fighting fatigue and unusually low muscle mass.

"Why does the house have eyes?" The words tightened in his throat, squeaking out, softer and higher than he intended. Far too meekly for a man who managed and, for years prior, worked on construction sites that stretched hundreds of years into the air. He could walk a beam ten stories up without regard for a safety harness, but couldn't look at a drawing?

Helena giggled. "Silly Daddy. All houses have eyes. That's how they see you and keep you safe. So I drew our house so it could see what it looked like."

"Oh, of course." Of course, she'd think that, or make herself think it. A child's imagination hard at work, creating angels to guide her when life seemed a little too chaotic.

Still, meeting the drawing's gaze, he didn't feel like angel was the right word.

"Can I take a nap, Daddy?" Her voice, half-muffled by her mouth against his chest. "I'm sleepy now."

"Yeah, sure," he said, almost distracted. Almost. He picked her up and tucked her into bed. For just a nap, she'd be fine in her regular clothes, and seemed too worn out to change anyway. This is normal, he told himself, normal fatigue for a girl who overcame extraordinary circumstances. Don't panic.

He kissed her forehead, drew the blinds, and walked to the door, shutting it behind him. As he left, he heard a creak and his daughter giggle. He told himself she was already dreaming. The rest? Shifting beams, loose boards. Nothing more than the house.

Chapter 5

Now that they didn't have to worry about hospital visits or playing catch-up on work, Charlotte and Elijah found it far easier to make dinner, keep up on chores, and do all the other miscellany required of homeowners. They'd been in their new home nearly a month, and he'd vacuumed the downstairs twice—every other weekend—and she'd even managed to check the boiler and furnace, just in case the realtor hadn't been entirely honest about upkeep and maintenance. She had been.

"I'm really surprised." Elijah spoke between spoonfuls of mashed potatoes. They sat at the kitchen table, happily chatting. Charlotte didn't seem to mind eating here despite the fact that, to his best understanding, her mother had died roughly two feet from where she now sat. "I mean, I know I shouldn't be, but I am anyway."

His beloved looked up from her asparagus. "What do you mean?" Helena's curious eyes turned on him, too.

"Maybe it's from moving around so much, you know? As a kid, I mean. Apartment to apartment, living out of a friend's basement, multi-family homes. Always something going wrong. Breaking. Blown furnace, shattered window, he… heck, one time, termites ate through the walls so bad our front door just fell out. Here, I know the realtors, former owners, everyone, really, took care of this place, but it seems weird to not need to fix anything. Even the wax seals on the toilets are perfect."

Helena giggled at 'toilet.' Charlotte laid her hand over his. Conveniently, he was left handed, while she used her right, allowing them to keep eating without breaking contact. They'd talked well into the night, early in their relationship, about their respective pasts. Neither liked keeping secrets in relationships, but each agreed full disclosure wasn't always easy—or an option.

"You okay?" She kept her probes light and cautious.

"Yeah. Makes me think, I guess, about how people don't appreciate their homes. But we're gonna take good care of this place, right, Monkeybutt?" Elijah made himself smile, eyes on his daughter.

Helena laughed again, her plate almost clear. A welcome sight, and not simply because she used to hate vegetables. "Yeah! And the house will take care of us."

"Right-o," he nodded. "It'll provide a roof for the rain, walls for the wind, windows for light, running water, electricity, heat… all those wonderful things." He'd trailed off a bit but snapped back to attention. "This year, I say *we* host Thanksgiving."

Charlotte's eyes flicked up toward the ceiling, for just an instant. He didn't even notice. "Are you sure?" she asked.

"Absolutely. It's always been my brother, or one of your sisters, or your parents. I say it's our turn—if not for a housewarming party, then at least to pay them back for their generosity in the past years. Besides, it'll be fun, cooking up a storm, having everyone talking, getting festive, ready for Christmas. What do you think?"

A moment of silence passed around the table. He looked at his wife, and followed her stare to Helena, who didn't look so cheery anymore, her fork poking at the table cloth and not the food she was so close to finishing.

"Not everyone." She didn't need to say more.

He stared down at his own unfinished meal, his stomach bottoming out—and not in a way that made room for the remaining steak. In the days after James's death, Charlotte and Elijah spent a lot of time online, trying to find healthy ways to grieve, for Helena if not for themselves. Most of what they found were arguments on who suffered the most: the siblings, the mother who birthed the child, or the partner who helped raise it. He scowled at such debates. Suffering isn't supposed to be a competition.

Still, he didn't have anything to say. His wisdom stopped there; it offered insight, but no solace. No doubt sensing his unease and inability to continue, Charlotte eased around the table, hugging her daughter.

"I know, sweetie. I know. We all miss him."

"If we'd moved first, I bet the house would've saved him." Helena's tiny frame produced a tiny voice, but they heard every word. "The house could've kept him healthy and safe!"

No sense in correcting her—not now, not here. Let her have her imagination as a buffer against the pain.

"Maybe you're right. Maybe if we moved, the house would've kept him safe. Life didn't work out that way, though. We might miss him, but he's in a safe place now, where he can't hurt anymore. That's why we're going to do our best to stay happy and healthy, like he would've wanted."

"Why didn't you get him better doctors?" Helena looked up, eyes overflowing. "Why did we go to that hospital and not a good one?"

"I know it's hard, but they saved you, Helena." She fell silent as Elijah tried to contribute, but emotional weight dragged him deep into the quicksand, his head already sinking beneath the surface. "We all miss him, but we have to move on. You have to do your best here, in this life, or else you get… stuck. Maybe someday you get *un*-stuck and come back as someone else. I'm not really sure. But we can't just go there. Life doesn't work like that."

"James wouldn't move on. Not without us." She delivered this last quip, then spoke no further. Her dislike etched itself along her face in lines too deep for someone so young, but she resigned herself to her parents' truth and returned to digging at her meal. None of it went in her mouth. Charlotte appreciated the feigned interest enough to start cleaning up. Dinner clearly ended with this conversation.

Elijah helped out, as much as he could, putting the salt, butter, and other items away while she took over the plates. They excused Helena, and she said thank you, keeping her manners no matter her mood, as they'd taught her.

That had been one of the interesting overlaps from their otherwise very different lives. Charlotte's foster family had always been very concerned with decorum:

what to wear, who to talk to, what body wash scents were and weren't permissible, and all the other finer points of high society. They weren't wealthy, but aspired to be, wanting to be ready when the time came. His parents, by contrast, moved from home to home, constantly and consistently evicted whenever the rent money ran out. They found it easier to pay the first month up front, then beg for extensions and mercy until kicked to the curb. With his mother at home raising five kids, and a father booted from freelance gig to freelance gig, they didn't exactly have an income, insurance, or a reliable car, beyond a busted-up hunk of metal almost as old as his parents.

These families shared one belief: all you are, in the end, is your name, so never act like anyone doesn't deserve your time. Every single person, ever, becomes worm food. Manners, eye contact, and a strong handshake would do more in the long run than anything else, and this idea, that no one is beyond respect or reproach, held some of the responsibility for how Charlotte and Elijah wound up together. It seemed fitting they pass these modes of behavior onto their child.

With this polite goodbye, Helena vanished from the kitchen, leaving the adults to stew in their guilt, a tar pit equal parts "We let one child die" and "We're failing the other." They knew, empirically, intellectually, that they couldn't do much more than provide love, support, and ways to keep her busy so she wouldn't dwell on James, but logic has never calmed a tempestuous heart, and nothing makes a heart storm like loss.

They cleaned in silence. Elijah didn't want to talk about family, and Charlotte didn't want to talk about death, but with nothing else on their minds, there wasn't much to say.

"You haven't been talking about work much lately. No new projects?" Her attempt at conversation, no matter how weak, beat his lack thereof by quite a bit.

"Overall, work's fine. Worried about scaling up productions a bit, but we'll manage. It's not like I'm the only person who sees a need for more workers, anyway. How's about your work?" He snorted out a quick laugh. "Seems like we haven't discussed either of our jobs lately."

She titled her head back and forth, a kind of column A, column B gesture. "Guess so, huh? Things are… okay. I mean, I disappeared for a while, not taking on new work because of… well, you know. But now that I'm back, all my old clients have swarmed out to help. I told them why I'd taken a break, and they're sending all sorts of work my way, and referring more clients, too. Way better than a GoFundMe page. I get to dictate the pricing."

"Changes per person?"

"No, even the jerks get the same price… but I always find a reason to recommend extra work." She smiled, showing off the slight gap by her right incisor. As her only dental flaw, it didn't require braces. On their third date, she stuck a toothpick in it for laughs. He still got a chuckle or two on the rare occasions she did it now.

"That's my wife: the consummate professional. Can't fix their attitude, so fix the game in your favor. Besides, I bet most of them think you're going the extra mile for 'em, don't they?"

"Oh, I make *such* a production out of it. 'A special offer, just because you're such a great client!' 'I'll lump this service under one bill.' 'The price of whatever, blah blah blah, because you deserve it.' I've had, maybe, two people ask if they were *really* getting a discount, and neither questions me further when I said, 'For you, I provide only the highest value, so every price is a discount.'" Charlotte rolled her eyes at the thought of her customers.

"You're so cheesy, I should serve you with wine." The kitchen sparkled, dishes cleared, sink emptied, dishwasher loaded, so he removed the placemats from the table and grabbed the spray cleaner.

She gave him a playful swat on the shoulder, laughing. Laughter had brought them together in the first place. All that talk about needing timing, chemistry, something in common—none of it means anything compared to a good sense of humor.

"Point is, everything's great. Good, and great. …Like you said, I'm a little surprised—but maybe more optimistic than you." Her tone teased, but her hand on his back said she knew how troubled he could be about good fortune.

Kissing her cheek, he said, "Well, we both have our insecurities, huh? Good thing they balance out."

"Yeah. If we both got lost in our heads about the same stuff, we'd never get anything done." She turned her eyes toward the rest of the house. "I'm going to see where Helena ran off to. Make sure she's okay."

Charlotte always told as much of the truth as she could stand, and yes, Helena bumbled through her mind as any five-year-old does. A child never fully escapes their parent's attention. Slips away for a moment, perhaps, but returns again just as quickly. On the slow walk up to her daughter's room, she turned to the slight creaks of the wall to her right, talking low.

"You're really okay with us hosting Thanksgiving here?"

Should I not be?

She shrugged, eyes upward to the two windows set high on the wall as she approached the front door. The stairs sat neatly off to the left of the living room—right, if just walking in—and she kept her gaze on the setting sunburned sky, blistering orange and red like the whole world had burst into flame, and only her family would survive, safe behind these walls.

"When I was little, no one thought you were real. I'd tell people, they'd say, 'You're making things up,' or 'You're just in shock.' This whole time, you were this little private piece of my life. Seemed like maybe you'd feel the same, in a weird way. Keep this house to us, and us alone."

It sounds like you're the one who'd rather not share.

A piece of lip skin tore off in her teeth before she realized she'd been biting. The voice never raised its volume, never adopted a harsher tone. It could be happy, or angry, or sad, without ever breaking stride. "I'm not sure what I want."

Oh?

She started up the stairs. "All this time, I dreamed of coming back here for closure. Now, you're real—I know you are, for certain—but that's all. I'm still just an orphan who feels out of place, like home is just a word for where I'm sleeping, not a place I want to be."

Home isn't a place you find. It's a hollow you carve out of the world.

"What do you mean?" No matter how slow she moved, she couldn't help being a few steps from the top.

I mean, you don't ask politely for a place to belong. If you feel out of place, demand that place make room for you. Don't worry and wait, don't sit around and hope things work out, stand up and say, "This. Is. Mine."

Charlotte reached the top and looked around, heart beating hard. Every door stood closed, the wood blocking sight, barring entry and exit. Her hands shook hard, barely gripping the rail.

Something wrong?

"It's just…" She cleared her throat. "Reminds me. Back then. When I couldn't get out."

Yet, the front door stays shut.

"Took a lot of therapy to get that far." Steeling herself, she circled the upstairs, opening each door all the way, and putting the doorstoppers in front of them. A rarely used and admittedly over-the-top way of avoiding this issue, a dozen or so rubber stops from the local hardware store had kept her secure in earlier years. They hadn't been necessary for a while, but this felt too weird.

Making sure to open Helena's door last, Charlotte eventually made it to her daughter's room, all her previous questions and queries forgotten. She found the girl pouring tea. Imaginary, of course, but playing hostess ranked among her favorite games. Being a good host went hand-in-hand with good manners, and she knew this was, on some level, an attempt to show her parents that she'd learned well.

"Sweetie?" She spoke from the doorway, not yet putting the stopper in place. "Do you know why the doors are shut?"

A tiny shrug. "To keep people out?"

Children could be so literal. "Oh, well, yes, but I meant the upstairs doors. All the doors up here were closed."

"I don't know." Her mouth set down in a forced line.

Crossing her arms, Charlotte probed further. "Are you sure? Because yours was shut too. You really didn't know your own door was shut?"

"Maybe one of my guests closed it on the way in." She gestured to her stuffed animals, which sat obediently around the table, as they always did. Actually, one seat went unfilled.

"Oh, did Mister Teddy do that? Or maybe Ducky here?" Stepping further into the room, she patted the head of a stuffed duck. Her daughter shook her head. She tried making eye contact, but Helena looked away, as she had at dinner.

Sighing, Charlotte unfolded her arms, sitting cross legged on the floor. "You okay?"

A nod.

"You know you can talk to me if something's bothering you, right?"

Another nod.

"So is there anything you'd like to discuss?"

As soon as she said it, she realized *discuss* had been the wrong word. Too formal, clinical, academic. A word they'd heard far too often from the doctors, and if Helena had been even slightly inclined toward answering, she visibly shut down. One hard shake of the head, eyes shutting, arms tight at her side.

Biting at her lips again, she uncoiled her legs, kissed the top of her daughter's head, and stood up. "Just be sure to keep the doors open, okay? You know Mommy doesn't like when they're shut."

She'd almost reached the door when a small voice said, "Why not?"

A fair question, and she deserved the truth. As much of the truth as Charlotte could stand, at any rate. She'd never told her before, in large part because she hadn't asked. Leaving the doors open had been a simple, unquestioned truth of her childhood, like when other parents tell their children that making funny faces will cause them to get stuck that way.

Turning back to the girl, she knelt down, doing her best to look her in the eye. "Well, when I was a little younger than you, my own mommy, the one who gave birth to me, was in an accident. She got hurt, and my daddy wasn't there, so I didn't know what to do. I tried to get outside to find him but couldn't get the door open. It scared me so much, that I still like making sure I can get out, just in case anything happens."

She screwed up her face for a second, thinking hard in the way only children can. "But you have a mommy."

"Oh, your grandma adopted me soon after. She saw me in the orphanage and said, 'She's special. We'll take her home.' That's how I got the family I have."

Helena looked past her, eyes drifting out of focus. "You mean… you can choose your family, and get a different mommy, or a baby, if you want?"

"Well, yes. There are people who make choices like that all the time. Family is about who you love and who you want to keep close. Not necessarily about who you're related to."

That answer seemed to satisfy her well enough. They talked for a little while longer about adoption and birth, but thankfully, she didn't have any questions that might've merited saying, "I'll tell you when you're older." All pretty innocent stuff.

This time, when Charlotte turned to go, no follow-up questions trailed after her. She did have one of her own, though. "Mind if I put the stopper in?"

Helena turned, looking up at her mother, eyes bright, with a big smile. "It's okay. I'll make sure it stays open."

She gave her daughter a proud grin back, thanked her, and started the walk back downstairs.

You've raised a good girl. Quiet, polite, inquisitive… you either wound up with a great family, or you've gotten very lucky.

"Can't it be both?" Charlotte whispered, glancing up to make sure no prying eyes watched from the railings.

I suppose, but usually, life is about one or the other. Something is, or it isn't. No gray areas. Let's assume you've simply done well. Passing on goodness to a child through genetics is a nice idea, but less flattering, and perhaps further from the truth.

"So you're saying I'm a good mother?" She'd take what compliments she could get.

What I'm saying, is that Helena is a good kid, just like you were. Then you lost your mom and had to leave. I'd hate to see that happen again, so take care of what you have while you still can. Children grow up quick. She won't be yours for much longer.

Chapter 6

They settled into their routine with a peculiar ease. Charlotte never lived on her own before, only ever with roommates, and from her experience, the first six to twelve months at any given place were rocky, fraught with little passive-aggressions as those who welcomed her into their lives also struggled to establish dominance. Vicky Peterson, her first-year roommate in college, had taken to "accidentally" letting her towel slip from her over-sized chest, and mentioning how her back ached from the counterbalance whenever they had male company (even gay male company—it wasn't about success). Her housemates, when she and three others split a place off-campus, never once warned each other when they were throwing parties, which led to two separate, simultaneous ragers taking place the night before her capstone course final. After breaking up with her post-college boyfriend and moving out of his place, into Chrystyna Anne's apartment, she'd have to keep her eyes on the floor to avoid stepping on the myriad tampon wrappers Chrystyna never bothered to throw away—but, according to the woman's boyfriend, this behavior hadn't been new.

Although, all of this went down far better than the high school debate team trip to Rome. She'd been paired with Julie Andrews, who vied constantly with Vicktorya Pherson for Hottest Girl in School, so she decided to celebrate her newly-eighteen status by slipping away from the class and bringing two men back to their hotel room. Mr. La Rouge answered a rather panicked phone call not long after. Thankfully, they'd only been robbed, and Charlotte hadn't exactly brought the Crown Jewels on that trip. Julie did get a senior superlative, but it was "Most Likely to Die Young," and the principal had to recall all the yearbooks. There were no reprintings.

"Honey?" Elijah waved a hand, snapping Charlotte from her reverie. "Did you get that?"

She blinked a few times and gave him the biggest, spaciest smile she could. "Nooooo, darling. Would you be so kind as to repeat yourself?"

"What?" He cocked his head.

"I… what do you mean, what? You asked, Did I get that?"

"No, I said *could* you get that." He pointed toward the front as the doorbell rang again. Elijah, busy prodding at the door to the crawlspace, had sunk to his elbows in tools and splinters.

Laughing at herself, Charlotte hurried across the living room, but Helena already answered the door. A burly man she didn't recognize, a little younger than her husband but a few inches and at least fifty pounds bigger, looked at her child through the screen door. His beard puffed out, bushy enough to hide all sorts of secrets.

"Hi!" Helena waved, as Charlotte's heart beat frantically at her bones.

"Hi there! Is your—oh, hello," he added, looking up. "Name's Maguire. I work with Elijah, he said I should come by."

"Oh!" She breathed a sigh and her worry vanished into the ether. "One moment." Turning back toward the kitchen, she called, "My wonderful husband, did you forget to mention a very large man intended to come by today?"

A clatter of metal and some choice swears echoed out of the pantry. As he approached, he gave a sheepish blush to her scowl, not needing another reminder about swearing around their daughter. He led introductions: Seamus Maguire works construction with him, overseeing the Cavanaugh estate restoration; Charlotte works in editing, freelance, doing damn well, sorry, darn well; Helena is five. All routine stuff.

The two talked shop for a while in the kitchen, mostly bits and pieces about odd goings on at the estate, equipment malfunctions, an electrical fire, all the other odds and ends, until they got to the real reason they needed to meet up: the restoration plans called for keeping the house exactly as it stood, but Seamus wanted to knock out walls in the third floor to turn some of the smaller bedrooms into suites with walk-in closets. They were getting paid by the work, not necessarily the job, so whatever they invoiced, they'd get paid for. Elijah shook his head hard at the idea.

Seamus pushed, but Elijah made it explicitly clear: don't deviate from the original plans. Restore the fixings, redo the wiring, repair the broken banister on the upper walkway, and shut the hell up.

"If you really want to knock something down," Elijah said, "help me bust open the crawl space. I've been trying to get in there, but I guess they sealed it over last time the place got worked over."

"Buzzsaw?"

"Nothing."

"Circular saw?"

"Can't get the angle right."

"Dynamite."

"My kid lives here, man. I'm not gonna blow up our own house."

Helena walked over and sat on the floor, looking up intently as they talked about different ways to get through the plaster. An intense look later, they had to admit it wouldn't open, coming to the conclusion it hadn't been sealed up, but filled in. The door couldn't move because there wasn't anywhere for it to go.

Charlotte took a place on the floor next to her daughter, watching her husband dig at the wall. "Funny how hard he's working to get in there, huh?"

A tiny shrug from her tiny daughter.

"You think he'll get in, or will Daddy give up?"

"Give up." The reply came swift. Immediate. A little cold. *Give up*—a suggestion, and an expectation. Not a guess. "The house isn't gonna let him in."

Leave it to a child to come up with such an imaginative extrapolation. Houses have doors and walls. They keep strangers out of their rooms, so of course, the house would forbid her husband from getting in the walls to inspect its guts. She almost chuckled at the thought. The house had guts, so why wouldn't it have eyes, too?

Charlotte looked at the walls. The house did, sort of, have eyes, just not in the way a child would mean. Not in the way anyone would mean. Giving her kid a smile, she wrapped her arm over her shoulder and pulled them close together, a small arm giving a reciprocal hug back.

"Maybe we'll let Daddy poke around a little while longer. Just for fun."

Helena finally tore her gaze away from the crawlspace door as she nodded. "Just for fun."

Chapter 7

Charlotte sat in her office, a glass of wine by her side as she ran through last-minute edits on yet another manuscript. Her eyes skimmed the page without focusing on the words, her brain having disengaged nearly an hour ago. Editing her edits didn't exactly thrill her. Yet, this decidedly dull portion of her job demanded itself attended to, lest she send out a document with mistakes. It wouldn't net her new business to make errors, considering she'd been hired to fix them.

"Finally," she mumbled as she reached the end, satisfied with her commentary. Based on her original notes, the novel hadn't been that good. Not a best seller, not even a mid-range read, nothing she'd suggest a friend pick up, but decent enough that maybe it'd get published by one of the newer independent presses. If she had the time and patience to figure out the printing and finalization parts, she could open up her own business, maybe hire others, but that didn't really appeal to her. Her adoptive father always said, "Find what you're good at, and do it until you're great. That's how you get ahead in this world."

She didn't need to get ahead. She had a husband, a daughter, and a home. Life brought challenges, of course, some she might never fully overcome. That didn't bother her. If anything, she'd be able to teach her daughter a valuable lesson: no matter what happened, you can keep going, and as long as you do, you'll be okay.

Charlotte sent the edits off to her client, then sat back, glass in hand. She rarely drank much, and tonight held up the same pattern: pour the glass, put it down, forget it until she finished working, then take a sip or two before returning to her family. Love or no, rituals have importance, and this moment of solitude served as her hibernation. Let the winter chill fade and emerge renewed into spring's bloom.

You're quiet tonight.

Faint creaks announced the voice's return. Charlotte wondered if she'd ever get a chance to see what it really looked like. For now, she felt comfortable just talking to it, reclining as she did, the way she might speak to an old friend while sitting on a porch, watching the sun set. If anything, it gave them a nice dynamic, she and this friend who'd never be fully present, but never be fully gone, either. Whenever she wanted to talk, the being listened; when she wanted privacy, she could hear it slink away.

"Yeah, been busy. Now I'm just thinking." She couldn't help but notice the solidity of real voices these days. Everyone, even Helena, had a heavy, meaty, guttural sense about their timbers, no matter how high and airy the voice itself might be. Resonating vocal cords created a thickness to their sounds that anchored them firmly in reality.

Did you find anything interesting while lost in thought?

This voice, though, the spirit, or person, or whatever, didn't sound like that at all. The whisper a rustle of barren branches, shook raw by late autumn's wind. Those rasps always brought her comfort. Maybe she had an unfair bias, as an October baby, but the upcoming Halloween, all the early darkness, brought her comfort. A therapist once told her this was a manifestation of trauma, that she only liked darkness because it made her feel like she could hide, but this was the same man who tried to tell her—at twelve—that she only liked books because it made her feel masculine and being a male would make her less weak.

"Not really. I think that's okay. It is okay, isn't it?"

To be dull?

"No, that's not what I meant. To be, I don't know, comfortable. To accept where you are, and not strive to change that. My husband and I both have good jobs, good income, a good daughter, and, well, I think things are okay where they are. Not great, obviously, but just that we'll be okay."

Accepting your lot in life, I see. Well, accepting a problem is the first step to overcoming it. So, I suppose congratulations are in order.

She creased her brow, pursing her lips. "What do you mean?"

Was that not your point? That your life's just okay, no better, and you're trying to think of ways you might improve them? You did lose a child not too long ago. I'd expect you to only be okay, but not to accept being only okay, if you can one day make things better.

Taking a sip of her wine, Charlotte said, "Loss like that isn't something you can fix overnight. Even if I could make things better, I don't know how."

Yes, precisely. That's what I said, and what I thought you meant. You were trying to think of the how. Apologies if it seems like I was trying to pry open a door.

Letting out a slow breath that rippled the dark liquid in her glass, Charlotte looked toward the ceiling, as if it might've suddenly taken the place of whatever god watched over her. "Sorry. Didn't mean to take an attitude. Wasn't your fault."

Either way, perhaps I should leave you to your devices.

"No!" she said, a little too loud, a little too quickly. "I… I never thought to ask you about your life. In there."

What about me could you want to know?

A fair enough question, and an issue she hadn't entirely thought through. This tether held her on one end and her past in the other, so she didn't want to piss if off. "What's it like in there? Are you, well, comfortable, or tired, or anything?"

In my earlier days here, I found myself colliding with pipes and beams, but never suffered pain for these missteps. Now, these paths are all I've known, and find they're so familiar that even walking through your rooms would feel alien to me.

What a life, stuck in somebody's walls. But that begged another question: "This place went through a few renovations. Didn't that involve knocking some walls out, or opening parts up? I guess you couldn't get out, huh?"

Evidently not.

A heavy, sardonic pause, where she could sense the being rolling its eyes.

Many workers opened many holes, but none served as doors between my existence and reality. I could press my hands toward open air, and strike a solid surface, as if it were still sealed. The workers didn't see or hear me.

"But you had a life before, right? …Did you? Are you a person?"

For a while, I recalled bits of my life. These fragments now escape me. I am whatever I've become. I locked away my old life, and threw away the key, as you might say.

Now for the big one, a question she had to ask, not that she wanted to. "So why can I talk to you, and what made others able to, too? What changed, what made me special, that you and I can have a conversation? If I'm really the only person still around who can talk to you, why?"

Before a reply could come, footsteps bounded down the hall behind her. The latch to her study door clicked shut. Whirling back, she saw her door closed, body racked by rolling thunder as a surge of adrenaline overtook her.

"Excuse me," she said, monotone, on autopilot, to the being in the walls. Charlotte crossed to the door, turned the knob, found it stuck, and recoiled. Shaking her hand, burned by this sudden aberration to her sense of normalcy, she turned the knob again and threw her shoulder into it, barely rattling the wood. Again, again, and something in her shoulder popped, so she cried out but didn't stop, tears stinging her eyes as she rammed into the door with what was almost certainly a dislocated shoulder.

It flew open so fast, she thought someone must have been on the other side, pushing to keep it shut, but she saw no one. Then she turned with fiery eyes toward her child's closed bedroom door.

Using her good arm, she turned the knob and shoved it open. Normally, she and Elijah knocked to give their five-year-old the pretense of privacy. To hell with that.

"Helena. Why did you shut my study door?"

Her daughter, who sat coloring at her tea table, looked up from her paper with big eyes—surprise and confusion eyes, or maybe just-got-caught eyes. She shrugged, letting out a noncommittal noise of denial that couldn't be held as an actual answer. The crayon in hand had ground down to a red nub.

Lips pressed into a line so thin and white it almost vanished against her face, Charlotte crossed the room, forcing herself to keep steady so as to not jostle her arm. Medical attention could wait. Disobedience couldn't.

"Helena," she said, louder, with a danger in her voice she'd never had to use on her before, "I'm asking nicely, because that door gets stuck, and Mommy got hurt trying to open it. Why did you shut the door?"

Another shrug. "Just playin'." She kept her eyes on her drawing.

"You were just playing?" When Charlotte had been Helena's age, she and a few other kids at the orphanage managed to sneak out a window onto the second story roof and took turns jumping off onto cars. Davey hadn't wanted to go, so Billy pushed him off, and he hit his head on a windshield. The caretakers kept saying Davey would be fine, but she never saw him or Billy again. All she could think of at the time was how glad she felt about having not jumped herself.

All things considered, she couldn't much fault Helena for playing so innocently. Telling her about her history in this house might've tripped a fuse in the kid's brain, making her play the way all kids do: energetically, with a dash of curious meanness, like how bullies pull pigtails just because they can, but pull harder if you cry.

"Okay." Charlotte breathed, in for a five count, out for a five count. "Okay. Just don't do it again. I think that door is broken."

Scribble, scribble, no eye contact, scribble. "Sorry, Mommy."

"It's fine, sweetie." Five-years-old, lost her brother, recently cheated death, no friends, new house. The girl had every right to play, even mischievously. It took all Charlotte's willpower not to chastise herself but managed to walk away without another word.

Cradling the injured arm with the good one, she made her way down the stairs and into the kitchen, where Elijah hustled around the kitchen, making "a special dish," the likes of which had entirely slipped her mind.

"Hey, Eli. I'm gonna run off to the hospital real quick. Need anything while I'm out?"

After a slight pause, he straightened up, turning around with a face marred by worry. "Hospital? The hell kinda books you editing up there?"

She snorted, shaking her head. "Our little darling got playful and decided to shut the door on me, but the damn thing jammed, and I couldn't open it. Threw my shoulder into it a few times to get out. I think I dislocated it."

"Once you're healed, we're sending you off to football camp to toughen you up," he said, pointing at her shoulder. "But, seriously, I'll drive you."

"I can drive!"

"Yes, my love, I know that, but how do you intend to change gears with your right arm out of commission?"

He had her there. All the independence and confidence in the world didn't mean a thing in the face of reason and inability. That left dinner to take care of, and bringing Helena to a hospital, which, after all she'd been through, might not sit too well, but they'd make it work. Elijah put the food off to another night, preserving what he could, then took the stairs two at a time to get Helena.

Creaks echoed their way down to her.

You okay?

"Fine. Like a four out of ten."

If I may... what's it like?

"What's what like? Pain?"

Yes. I don't recall. All these years, I've never felt it. Would you care to indulge me?

She glanced up toward the sound of her husband and Helena bustling around her room. "Pain comes in many forms. This is a sharp ache, two things feeling separate, with little lightning bolts arcing out every time they shift or grind together. It's an electricity. Think of a broken support beam that splinters a bit every time the house shifts and makes the halves bump each other. Does that clarify pain?"

I suppose. If you're in pain again, I may ask again, since there are different kinds.

Already annoyed without the supernatural game of twenty questions, she snapped, "Why do you care?"

You got me thinking, if I were human long ago, then perhaps I can be human again someday. I don't want to be caught off guard if that happens.

Her mom always said to keep your problems in perspective, because somebody has it worse. Well, that somebody lived under her roof—or inside it, she supposed—and served as a damn good reminder that a busted-up shoulder wouldn't kill her. Elijah had great insurance, too. They'd be fine.

"I'm sorry about you being trapped the way you are. For whatever that's worth."

And I'm sorry about your shoulder.

"Thanks," she whispered as her husband returned. He threw a large coat over her shoulders, so she wouldn't get too cold, then made for the front door. This one, thankfully, opened.

Chapter 8

Paulina couldn't shut up, ever, except when she healed people. Elijah never put much faith in reiki, or spirit healing, or whatever the hell else she called it, but Charlotte's shoulder had been giving her quite a bit of grief. Doctor Smith, the physiologist she wound up seeing for the dislocation and sprained rotator cuff, said this injury could take months to heal. As a good husband, Elijah wouldn't stand in the way of whatever New Age voodoo she and her friends wanted to try in the name of getting better. If it worked, excellent. If not, well, maybe the placebo effect could help out a bit.

Of course, this meant privacy, so Pauline offered to provide the treatment in the master bedroom, allowing Elijah and Helena to do as they pleased downstairs. Overall, he didn't much mind. Moving ranked as one of the most stressful events somebody can go through and moving back to the house where Charlotte watched her mother die couldn't have been easy on her, even if she kept her smile up and kept saying everything's great.

"Great" wouldn't have led to her nearly tearing her rotator cuff slamming herself against an unlocked door. A little mindfulness, meditation, mind-connection, whatever Paulina called it wouldn't be too bad of an idea. Even if all it did was get her to lie back and shut her eyes for a while, that'd be enough.

With Helena explicitly clear on not bothering Mommy, who'd be upstairs with Paulina for around an hour, he went down into the basement to organize. They'd agreed to keep everything boxed up for the time being, but he knew she didn't like doing that. As long as he didn't start throwing the extra pots and pans around, or generally make any kind of huge racket, he could take this job off their joint queue without putting an extra burden on her.

Ultimately, he only managed to find forty minutes worth of work. Once he went through the gardening supplies, power tools, and spare electronics they'd finished out of the storage unit, he found himself facing the kitchenware and Christmas decorations. As far as holidays were concerned, all that stuff could and should stay boxed up for simplicity's sake. Unpacking decorations ahead of time is the one major instance where 'organizing' actually creates a bigger mess. Nobody needs a thousand tiny plastic spiders scattered on the floor, or tinsel getting mixed in with the laundry. Pots, pans, spare cutlery, and all the miscellany they used for cooking stayed where they'd put it, only because he didn't feel like dragging the box to the kitchen and making a huge racket.

Slightly sweaty and very dusty, Elijah brushed himself off, looking at all his arguably hard work. Where there had been a dozen or so cardboard boxes, they now had empty space, revealing more of the nicely tiled floor, which would surely shine if he vacuumed away the dust and debris they'd tracked in during the move. The rafters needed a dusting, because beyond the laundry machines, which sat patiently just a few feet from the stairs, waiting for their next loads, they really hadn't been down here much. It could make a great play area for Helena when she got older and wanted a place she could hang out with friends that didn't involve her parents traipsing through at any given moment.

"But no boys," he muttered to himself. "No boys allowed in the basement, where we can't keep an eye on what they're doing." He tapped his chin. "Or... or girls, either, if she's... Well, we can't say 'no one else allowed,' that's not fair. Whatever." Any such decisions were at least—hopefully—ten years off, so until then, he'd focus on keeping the basement clean and functional.

The guys at work might badger him about not setting up a Man Cave, but he'd never been the type to need one. Besides, who would he have over? Seamus's one visit marked the only time in nearly six months that a guy had come around with the intention of only talking to him, and that had been a work-related visit, too. Otherwise, all their guests were friends of his *and* Charlotte's, so they all talked together.

Brushing his hands against his pants to avoid tracking much dust back upstairs he ascended the rickety steps, mentally noting to fix them soon. Helena sat at the kitchen table, coloring, and humming a tune he didn't recognize.

"Hey, Monkeybutt, watchya coloring?"

She turned around, all bright eyes and sweet smile, waving as if seeing him from far off, not ten feet. A smile broke itself across his face, seeing her so exuberant, finally getting her strength and energy back.

"Hi, Daddy!" It didn't matter that she didn't answer the question. Having helped raise two of his siblings, he knew how quickly the young could shift the entirety of their attention span. Doubly so when the new focus was someone they cared about.

He walked over, giving her a big smooch on the top of her head, partially as a way of seeing what she'd drawn without drawing attention. It looked like a closet, a door opening to a small space with clothing inside— and someone in there, slumped forward, yet not falling. Other lines suggested walls, floors, carpeting, all the normal elements a room should have, except for what appeared to be a more or less literal skeleton in the closet.

"What's this?" Elijah reached over, tapping the paper. He did his best to keep his tone neutral. If kids don't think they've done anything wrong, they're usually happy to talk about whatever they've been up to.

"It's my picture I drew. Do you like it?"

How was he supposed to answer that question? "I do. You're so talented! But who is this, and what's he doing?"

She looked back, as if having forgotten. "That's Davey Sanderson. He was a banker. He had lots and lots of money, so much money! You could eat his money until you exploded, and he'd still have so much!" Her arms shot out wide to illustrate the explosion, then wider still to refer to his horde.

"Oh, that's no good! I don't want to explode."

"That's okay, Daddy. He's dead now. He doesn't have any money. He did bad stuff to get it, so it all went away, and Davey didn't want to go to prison. He hid in the closet instead."

Elijah bit at his lip. "Why did he hide in there?"

"Because! Davey wore suits, and suits have ties. He hung there until he died so he didn't have to go to prison. Duh." Duh, a quick, snide little jab, because of course he committed suicide, silly Daddy, what else do you do when guilty of embezzlement and fraud?

Parenting already brought him so many critical moments where, unsure of the right move, he made a decision that he ultimately hated, or at the very least felt had been dead wrong. Decisions he'd have to live with for a long, long time. This might've been a comparatively minor one but seeing the innocent way she scribbled at her paper, putting up a picture frame a few feet from the hanged man in the closet, then filling it in with swirly, swooping lines that could've almost been art, he didn't have the courage to criticize the morbidity. Still, where the hell had she gotten *that* from?

Kids always get weirdness from somewhere. Mom almost stopped taling his brother, Luis, to church after the pastor described Cain and Abel. The next day, Luis tried to hit him in the head with a brick. Luckily, he'd been too young to wield it effectively, but still, he hadn't intended to be violent. Just acting out something he'd seen before. So where had Helena heard about fraud, or embezzlement, or suicide?

"You're very imaginative, sweetie." He patted her head. "Do you want to be an artist when you grow up?"

"I don't know." She looked thoughtful for a second, then changed her mind. "No, I don't want to be an artist. I want to be a house."

"…A house?"

"Yup! I want to be a house, so I can keep people safe. I'll cover them from rain, and keep them warm when it's cold, and they'll be so happy to have me as their house. I'll be the best house in the whole world!"

He laughed. "Okay. How are you gonna become a house?"

Helena shrugged, looking around. "The same way everyone else becomes houses!"

Elijah smiled. She really did have a great imagination. Maybe writer would make a better career for her than artist. "Don't want to be a doctor, or police officer, or fire fighter? They protect people too."

She shook her head. "House. I want to be a house."

"You got it. House it is. The next time I see a recruiter asking if people are interested in becoming houses, I'll make sure to tell them all about you. We'll set you up with an internship, so maybe you can start as an apartment first, then work your way up."

A vacant, unblinking gaze met his. "What's a… a interships?"

"It's like a tiny job. A job for tiny people, like you, Monkeybutt."

Voices sounded from upstairs, so apparently the reiki session ended. He walked off to talk to the women about how it went. Even if he didn't believe it worked, he still cared about whether Charlotte *felt* like it worked.

Helena sat at the table a moment longer, then, when her father had left, she turned her eyes toward the ceiling.

It's such a pretty picture. You really are a talented artist, but your mother will be coming down soon. You saw how your father was. She might not understand how talented you are either. Why don't you take it upstairs and tuck it away with the others, so they stay our little secret?

With a smile, she whispered back, "Okay."

She crept up the stairs a moment after her father, but while he walked into the Master bedroom, she walked into her own. She tucked Davey Sanderson into the pile she stashed under her mattress with the others, then tooled off, her suicide sketch already forgotten.

Chapter 9

Charlotte tucked Helena into bed with a kiss on her cheek. They'd all had a long day of errands, running around, and playing Chutes and Ladders, but she'd be remiss if she didn't offer her daughter a bedtime story. As always, she accepted. Lacking the energy for originality, she launched into an old favorite about a princess who got swept away after a rainstorm caused the river to flood. She hardly got to her unceremonious landing in The Rat Forest before Helena's eyes drifted shut.

"Well, we knew that was coming, didn't we?" Charlotte stood up, grimacing as her knees creaked in protest, and made her way to the door, flicking the lights off.

A few days earlier, Helena made a huge step toward adulthood, asking if she could leave the nightlight off, too. This surprised both her parents. They figured, after the trauma of her illness and losing her brother, she'd sleep with it on for a long time. Those first few weeks, she'd had terrible dreams. Not even nightmares, necessarily—some were scary, sure, but others, she woke up crying. Charlotte dealt with these. She knew he wouldn't admit or acknowledge it, but she'd caught Elijah having a few of those too. Late night trips to the bathroom, where he stood in front of the mirror, wiping tears off his cheeks, trying to regain control of his breathing.

Masculinity may have been stupid to her, but his family considered 'being a man' important. She didn't know where in the Bro Code it said that a man couldn't cry at losing his son, or even at a tragic dream. With some exceptions, people don't control their dreams, so whatever played in his mind's movies couldn't really be his fault. Still, she pretended not to notice, lying in bed with her eyes shut, because sometimes, leaving him alone was the kindest option.

Charlotte walked downstairs, not hearing any telltale creaking from the walls. The being must have been resting, or whatever it did when not watching them. It raised so many questions, but she had no reason to assume it lied when it claimed it really didn't know how it got there, or why, or how to escape the walls. She didn't know enough about dimensions or sciences or the supernatural to speculate, either. It could've been a weird ghost, a demon, an interdimensional traveler who made some pretty huge errors, or just a regular person in a strange situation. Either way, she liked having it around. She finally knew about her mother's death—the real version, not the tabloid 'domestic abuse manslaughter' version all the police and papers ran with.

Down in the kitchen, Elijah sat doing Sudoku, as he so often did. This was the only activity he could really engage at night without also keeping himself awake. "Hi, honey. She all tucked in?" He looked up, peering at her in a slightly out-of-focus way she remembered from her brother in the months before he finally got glasses. Neither she nor Elijah were old by any means, but perhaps the time had come to make him go to an ophthalmologist.

"Yup, all snug up in her bed. You've been paying the bills, right?"

"Of course. Why do you ask?" A brow crept up toward his hairline.

She chuckled. "In all the excitement, I'd completely forgotten. Are we okay? I mean, between mortgage, utilities, taxes, all that, we have a lot more bills now than we used to. At least, I imagine we do. We're not going broke or anything?"

"Nope." He gave one solid shake of his head. "I'd've mentioned it if we were."

"Oh, good. So, as far as a budget goes, we're still okay, still saving and all that?"

"Yup. Putting a nice amount aside each month, even after our IRA contributions. Our Roths are both maxed for the year, and your SEP is getting close."

Charlotte leaned across the table to give him a kiss. "You're so wonderful."

"Because I'm good with money?" He teased. "I hope you haven't stayed just for my massive fortune."

"Because I never have to worry about money. My parents—the ones who adopted me—were always talking about needing a job because inflation this, investment that, stuff about stocks and savings bonds and certificates of deposits, all sorts of jargon I never really understood. They made it out like I'd wind up in the gutter if I didn't catch on quick, but I guess it's true, what they say about how English majors suck in STEM fields. Never really got the hang of this Wall Street stuff. Too complicated, I guess."

Elijah shrugged, waving her off. "Not that complicated. I mean, apps these days really simplify things, so between Stash, Acorn, Wealthsimple—"

"Babe, you're losing me."

"Er, they give you access to easy portfolio management, so you can decide what kind of risk profile and asset allocation you want, while controlling what micro ETFs you purchase, along with tax loss harvesting and—"

She pressed a finger to his lips. "I get it. Your credit score is amazing. But, darling? I have no idea what you're saying."

A goofy smile splayed out across his face. She'd fallen in love with that smile. She admired all the serious, hardworking qualities about him, but that little inner goofball, the faint echoes back to the child he'd never fully gotten to be, that side of him won her over. Anybody can learn to be a go get 'em type, pull themselves up by the bootstraps, work hard, earn money. Anywhere she went in the world, every industry had tons of those types. There weren't a lot of guys who could be as industrious as Elijah and still retain that boyish appreciation for just being alive. Even after all that talk of investment finances, he grinned around her finger like he'd been caught hiding frogs in his bedroom after a long day down by the river.

"Point is, we're good. Don't you worry at all, my love." He kept his lips smushed against her fingertip, muffling his words a little. That didn't matter much. She'd always know what he meant.

They stayed up a while longer, talking quietly in the kitchen, not aware of the fact that Helena never went to sleep. Bored with Mommy's old stories, she'd shut her eyes, waiting until she stopped talking about Princess Gwen and all the stupid, smelly rats on the outskirts of her kingdom. Every story her mom told had a moral lesson tacked on, and they didn't make her tired anymore, unless she counted how tired she'd gotten of the snooty endings.

Would you like another one of my bedtime stories?

The House had far better stories. New, fresh tales, full of excitement and mystery, without any need to tell Helena how she should act in the brighter hours. They made her feel like the older kids in the few cartoons her parents let her watch—the ones who'd sit around telling ghost stories to scare the main characters. They didn't scare her, though. That's what Mommy and Daddy didn't understand. She'd almost died. She watched James die. *That* had been scary. A story? Never. Little princess stories didn't mean a thing to her now.

"Okay." Helena whispered toward the ceiling, not exactly sure which part of The House watched her tonight.

An old one, or a new one?

She'd asked to hear a few stories more than once, but tonight, she wanted something fresher. Original. Previously unheard. The kind she could scare other kids with, once she grew old enough to tell these stories herself.

"Can you tell me a new one?"

Of course. I have so many stories, I'm not sure I'll ever be able to tell you all of them.

This made her positively giddy, and she snuggled down tighter in her covers, ready for tonight's tale.

Once, a man named Tyler Travitz lived here with his fiancée, Mila Nilopolis. They moved in one day in late

July, planning to get married in November. When they first walked in my doors, Tyler dripped sweat, because it had already been a very hot summer, and on top of that, he had to move all the furniture. Mila entered first, though. She held the keys, and nothing else. Her beloved insisted that she not have to lift a finger, not that she had any intention of helping. Everything about her had been perfectly placed. Her new nails, shiny and pink, fixed her freshly cut hair in a compact mirror. All she spoke about was how far of a drive it would be to her old salon, and she didn't know if it'd be worth it to find a new one nearby.

"What if these people don't know what they're doing?" She kept looking in the mirror, talking without caring if her groom-to-be could hear.

"What people?" His chest heaved. The couch he'd just shoved through the front door should've been handled by two people, but everyone knows a princess isn't a real person. She couldn't have helped, even if she tried. She wouldn't have known how.

"The salon!" She scowled at him. "Are you listening?"

"Sorry, yes, of course. The salon. Why wouldn't other places know?"

She held out her hand, flashing her nails at him. "Do you think just any old place could do this?"

Now, I could tell from the look on his face that he had no idea what made her nails so special. They were a single color, glossy but otherwise unremarkable, and really, I couldn't tell what made them special either. But, he knew there was a right answer, because he nodded. "Oh, well, obviously, you can't just expect any old place to do that."

"See? You do understand." Mila smiled, then let him *bring the rest of the furniture in without trouble, up until the vanity. She had a big dresser, heavy as could be, with a giant mirror on top. Some said the mirror was so big, that if you looked too close, you'd see the whole world, but you'd get stuck in the reflection. People aren't supposed to see that much.*

That... That's how you get stuck.

The House faltered. Helena pulled the covers down, just a little, to look around. The House didn't usually hesitate, or get hung up, or anything. She had an odd feeling like it might need a hug, but didn't know how to make her arms that long.

"Are you okay?" she squeaked.

Oh. Yes, sorry. Where was I...? When he brought the vanity in, he bumped it on the door, leaving a tiny scratch on the frame, so she flew into a rage. "Why don't you care about my things?" She yelled so loud, the whole city could hear her. "It's like you want me to be miserable!"

He never once yelled back, or argued, or objected, or complained. That's what a good husband does, or so he believed. Tyler said that into the bathroom mirror every single night: a good husband carries all the burdens, so his wife doesn't have to.

But on that first day, he moved furniture while she yelled, and he unpacked boxes while she screamed, and he organized the house while she insulted him. "Pathetic!" she spat. "You embarrass me! I hope you know how lucky you are that I'm marrying you!"

By that evening, she'd lost her voice, and all he had left to move was the vanity.

"Do you mind if I don't move this tonight?" His voice came out smaller than ever. So small, it almost

disappeared and took him with it. "I just want to make sure I don't bump it on the way. I'll move it soon, when I'm refreshed and strong."

She waved him away, so he got in the shower and cried. He cried so hard he didn't think he'd ever stop. Water washed away his tears, curling over his cheeks and rubbing his back, warm and gentle, the way a more loving wife would. The water helped Tyler realize he shouldn't be crying. There were plenty of ways to handle this without him having to ever shed another tear.

Mila had all sorts of pills to help her deal with princess problems, and that night, Tyler took them all. Every single pill. She didn't think it strange that he laid perfectly still on their bed all evening, but when she found her jars empty, she almost started to rage again. This time, she yelled, and he didn't even move. He couldn't respond. She called 9-1-1, screaming much different now. He died there before the ambulance arrived.

The princess wasn't sure how to live without a prince, but that didn't matter. She had her nice house here to help her, and that's exactly what I did.

"You always thought he was weak," I told her. "You yelled at him for it. Why cry, when you can prove how strong you really are?"

She liked that idea. She nodded, smiled, stood up tall and pretended she knew what she was doing. "Okay. I'll be strong. I didn't need him, right? I'm the strongest person I know!"

The vanity still waited in the living room to be placed somewhere special, and she loved the idea of having a personal boutique upstairs. A room reserved for make-up and beauty. A room reserved for her. Taking hold, she eased the vanity up the stairs, one step at a time, grunting and sweating as she went. She broke two nails, feeling them splinter, then crack so badly they started to bleed, but she had no one to yell at. She knew better than to yell at her house. No one should ever yell at their house.

Mila believed she was strong, but strong people don't need to yell at those they love. They don't need to insult and belittle others to feel big. She never made it to the top. Her arms weren't strong enough, because she never once carried her own weight in this world. She didn't have the stamina for hard work, because she'd never worked hard before.

Falling backward, she tumbled down the stairs, and the vanity came rushing after. It crushed her at the bottom, the weight breaking the bones in her chest and pressing down on her tiny heart, making it difficult to breathe. She gasped, blood on her lips, spraying out with every feeble cough, but that didn't matter much. What mattered was that the vanity landed so the mirror was right over her face. She looked deep into it, and for the first time in years, she had to look herself in the eye. No examining her acne, no applying foundation, no keeping lipstick inside the lines. Mila came face-to-face with the whole world, including what she'd been hiding away beneath the make-up. That's what really killed her. The princess looked inside herself and saw absolutely nothing.

Helena looked up with wide eyes, trying to hide an excited smile. "Did she get stuck?"

Oh, yes. When people finally found her, they were too concerned with her body to notice she stayed in the mirror. Now she pretends to be reflections, so she can learn a little about what it's like to be a person, so look close. Next time you see yourself in a mirror, it might actually be her, pretending.

"What happens if she keeps pretending?" She gripped the covers tight, talking just a little too loud.

Hush, child. It's getting late, and that's a story for another time. I'll tell you soon. For now, you should be getting to sleep.

That seemed like a terrible idea, but she didn't argue with The House. After all, it knew everything, and wouldn't tell her more stories if she made it mad. Helena blew it a kiss goodnight, curled up, and slept, dreaming of her reflection watching her from behind the glass.

Chapter 10

Charlotte sat at the kitchen table massaging her shoulder while Elijah fixed his costume. Halloween came upon them far faster than anticipated, and they realized too late that suburban life comes with certain expectations. Namely, that they'd shell out a crapload of money to dress up in cheap polyester and throw sugary snacks at children who'd probably never once be grateful for the candy. After all, they were all part of the Halloween cycle, and the holiday didn't simply expect, but demanded, that these children be given junk food. They were *owed* the extra pounds, the pre-diabetes, the hyperactivity followed by inevitable nausea and lethargy as their bodies attempted to process the toxic amount of glucose coursing through their blood.

"Okay, I get it, you don't like Halloween." Elijah laughed, only partly due to awkward nervousness.

"I mean, it's not that I *hate* it, just that I kind of forgot about it. The major events of my year go: back-to-school day, Nine-Eleven, Indigenous Peoples Day, then there's this big gap until Thanksgiving." Her fingers dug at the soft tissues, avoiding the loosely strung gauze she'd wrapped around herself. The mummy costume had been, in part, an excuse to throw her arm in a sling if the night really wore on.

"What about the premiere of *Stranger Things* season two? Surely that was a reason to mark Halloween on the calendar."

"Yeah, I marked the *date,* but I still put the holiday out of my mind. Besides, we lived at an apartment! People never trick-or-treat at apartments, and decorating is on a tenant-by-tenant basis. I've never seen a landlord or manager decorate the actual building. It's easy to forget."

He shrugged, seeing no point in continuing the conversation. She had her funny little hang-ups. This ranked among her least harmful, so if all this meant was a slightly sour attitude, it'd be alright. Besides, she wouldn't ruin the night for Helena. Absolutely not.

With a final flourish, he secured his cape, fake fangs in place. "Blah!" He spoke in the cheesiest possible Dracula impression, on purpose, to at least pretend to join in on her distaste for the day. A good husband at least feigns support for his wife, just as a good wife doesn't let him catch her shaking her head when he's doing something unnecessarily macho and patently stupid.

"Helena! Are you ready?" Charlotte called, then paused for a moment. She turned to her husband with a quizzical look. "You helped her with the costume, right? What did she wind up dressing as? I've been so preoccupied with physical therapy and not caring about Halloween that I didn't even think of her costume."

Elijah hid behind his cloak, drawing it cheesily over his hunched form, then peeking out from the hem. "I do not know vat she vanted to be!" Then, more seriously, "I thought that you had it covered. She asked me to bring home cardboard to help make her costume. That's it."

She stared at him so hard she almost forgot to react. The problem with some men is that, once they get an idea in their head, it's impossible for them to consider other options. Sure, some were exceptions to this rule, but Elijah wasn't. When he proposed, he'd been so focused on taking the knee in the park where they'd had their first date that he dragged them both out in a torrential downpour, where the ring nearly vanished into a storm drain when a heavy gust knocked it from his slippery hands.

Tonight held a far different problem. "Didn't she ask about utility scissors and super glue? And you mean to tell me she's up in her room making her costume… by herself?"

They held each other's gaze for a moment, then bolted in unison for the stairs. She ran as best she could with her injury, which still sent little bolts of pain through her from the bouncing motion. Working in construction left Elijah reasonably fit, though. He beat her to the stairs, then took them two at a time, cape billowing out with a B-movie flair, cheap material fluttering stiffly from his haste.

She arrived to find him in Helena's doorway, staring into her room. This was it. He'd stopped from horror, Helena having accidentally cut herself to pieces, then glued them back in the wrong spots like some kind of cubist cenobite. "What's wrong?" Not that she wanted to know.

"Nothing, just… where is she?"

This might've been worse. "What do you mean, where is she? Move!" She shoulder-checked him with her good arm, motherly rage quickly blotting out concern for her slow-to-react husband, only to find a pretty obvious answer to his question.

Her room almost appeared normal, without any scraps of paper or cardboard spotting the carpet. Tea cups sat along her table, stuffed creatures in place, all looking toward the one empty seat that, her parents agreed, she'd left open for James, as a way of not letting him go. Tightly drawn sheets held snug to her bed, like it had never been slept in. Dolls and dusty toys leered from the shelves, resentful of their wasted life, unfulfilled due to the child's lack of desire to play with them. Rose-tinted walls glowered with a faint crimson from the light of the late afternoon sun.

In the center of all this sat a house. Well, not a house, but *the* house. Theirs. The one they were currently inside, scaled large enough that it could be 'worn' by a small person. Paint sloped in sloppy lines all around the exterior, matching the siding, and pencil-drawn shingles pockmarked the roof. On the front rested two windows, the eyes to the house, and behind them, her daughter's shiny green eyes peered out, alight with mischief.

Kneeling down in front of her daughter and this 'costume,' she looked inside the house and put on her best fake smirk to conceal the brief, overwhelming panic that consumes any parent who loses track of their child for more than twelve seconds. Helena didn't need to feel guilty over this, and certainly didn't deserve any kind of punishment or freak-out. She'd have a talk with Elijah later, one hell of an angry, quiet, 'don't let our daughter hear how pissed I am at you right now' talk, but that could wait.

"What do we have here, hm?" Charlotte said. "Is Helena going trick-or-treating as the lady of the house?"

A peal of giggles burst from Helena's cardboard confinement, eliciting an "Ohhh," of realization from her father. "No, Mommy, I'm just the house."

"Just the house, huh? What made you want to go as…" Realization knocked the wind from her. It stopped her heart, then surprise kickstarted it again. Helena could hear it. She could hear the voice of the house, talk with the presence that lived here, and probably had been the whole time. Charlotte turned her head to the empty seat at Helena's tea table. "…As the house?"

"Because! No one goes as their house. But our house is nice, so I'm the house today." Her voice muffled a bit through the thin fake walls, but she heard every word, loud and clear.

Elijah walked over, kneeling by her side. "Well, isn't our little Monkeybutt creative? I think this is a lovely costume."

"Shut up, Eli," Charlotte whispered. The House creaked and groaned, a few long footsteps circling the room's perimeter. "Sweetie, how are you going to walk?"

Helena stood up, lower body sticking out of the bottom. There clearly weren't floors. The lower edge sat low enough that she still couldn't really use her arms, but the front door flapped open and shut. Presumably, this served to let her get treats. "With my legs."

Forcing a smile, she ignored her husband's perturbed glance. "Well, we've got a lot of neighborhood to cover, so we better get out there before all the good candy's gone! I'll even hold the bag, so you can just focus on—

on being the house." The words caught in her throat, not wanting to be said, as much as she didn't want to say them. Not too loudly, anyway.

She didn't mind talking to it. She always allowed for the remote possibility that it really had been her imagination, and the stress of moving back here caused her to have a mild psychotic break. Now, she couldn't decide which was worse: the idea that something had been trapped in the walls of this house, or that it had been spending so much time with her daughter.

"Yay! Halloween!" Helena cheered, bumbling for the door, only to smack into the doorframe.

"C'mon, kiddo, let me guide you down the stairs. Put your arm out the door so you can take mine." Charlotte stepped in front of her daughter and led her away, with Elijah bringing up the rear.

They'd talk outside. Quietly, without Helena hearing, so she wouldn't worry. Worry should be reserved for adults, who had kids to watch out for, and bills to pay, and knew that houses weren't supposed to have a thousand eyes lurking in its shadows.

Chapter 11

Charlotte hadn't ever been in this situation before. *No one* had ever dealt with another person—or whatever it was—living in their house's walls, that she could assume pretty easily, but for her, the newness came down to her lack of awareness. Her foster parents always bragged about her situational awareness, about how nothing ever escaped her attention. It got to the point that they started calling *Where's Waldo?* "There's Waldo" instead. She got fives on four different AP tests largely because she could spot the trick answers and eliminate almost every choice, leaving only the correct answer. In college, two of her closest friends stopped inviting her to their monthly Escape Room excursions because she could solve them so quickly. She totally understood and didn't mind at all. The manager even offered her a job designing their newest room, which wound up being so difficult, every other group had to forfeit.

Her middle name could've been awareness. No one would've questioned it. Now, she felt uncertain. Unsteady. She didn't live up to her imaginary namesake anymore, because a being in her walls had been talking with her child for months, and she'd had no idea. Charlotte focused so intently on *her* relationship with this presence that she paid no mind to the one it formed with her daughter, and she wasn't sure which was hitting her worse: being a bad parent or being so blind.

Do you not trust me?

Its whisper stayed the same, as airy as always, yet her perception of it shifted. She'd once felt it to be the wind through leafless branches in the later seasons, but now, it seemed to be the cold itself. Not the gentle rustle of a breeze, but the harsh snap of New England winter, sending a chill through her she knew she'd never fully shake off.

"It's not about trust." She paced the basement, talking to the walls. Down here, surrounded by brick and cement, she couldn't be sure where It resided unless in the ceiling, directly above her. Mortar doesn't creak and groan the way wood and plaster does. But, the sound of the laundry machines chugging and churning away muffled her a bit, so she could speak more directly without fear of anyone overhearing. Well, without fear of Elijah overhearing. As far as Helena went, she apparently already knew their house's big secret.

"It's not about trust." Her attempts to formulate actual thoughts about this failed, but she pressed on. "It's about the fact that neither of you told me. I mean, I'm her mother, and she didn't think to mention hearing you?"

She's a child. By your own admission, she's never lived in a house before, and has quite the active imagination. Every time she brought me up, or mentioned The House watching over her family, you and your husband both brushed it off as the ramblings of a child. I believe, when she said, 'the house' could've kept your other child from passing away, you even said, 'Maybe if we moved, the house would've kept him safe.' She did mention me. Plenty of times. You simply didn't think others could hear me, too, so you told yourself she was just making things up.

Damn. It had a point. She couldn't very well have expected to engage Helena in an open dialogue about the god damn house talking to them both if every time her child brought it up, she brushed it off as being playful.

"I'm her mother! I expect at least a little honesty, a little disclosure, about circumstances like this. She could've explained, told us about actually hearing you, but instead she skipped all the details." Elijah in particular cared quite a bit about honesty. He'd worked hard to instill her with that value, and it had been for nothing.

Honesty? She was honest. As honest as you were, when you were her age, and told the responders, the case workers, and your eventual foster family about how a person living in the walls had helped you. How 'the house' had a voice, and it guided you to safety. They disregarded everything you said, just as you disregarded her. This has nothing to do with honesty. You're both simply following the pattern your life established long ago.

She paced faster, footsteps scuffing the oddly dirty floor, which she made a mental note to vacuum sometime this week, or at the very least before

Thanksgiving, assuming they'd still have the celebration here in their bizarre house, not that she'd actually remember, because it ranked absolute dead last on the list of things she could give a shit about right now. Knots in her hair latched onto her fingers as they raked across her scalp, but she didn't notice little tangles of loose strands falling free, joining the dust bunnies below.

This couldn't be happening. She'd been so miserable as a kid, being told again and again that she imagined the voice that saved her life, she swore she'd always believe in the supernatural. Yetis, zombies, Baba Yaga, the Wendigo, whatever the stories said, she left a little room in her heart for them to be true. She never went to church or joined a religion because she believed all of them had a little truth and didn't want to decide one was more right than another. Charlotte believed in Santa until she was twelve.

Then, when it mattered, she hadn't even *considered* the supernatural option. Despite talking to this being on a daily basis, she'd become the skeptic, the rationalist, the logician, the same tired old adult who told herself that her kid liked to make up weird ideas, because kids were kids and needed stories to fill the silence of their job-less, bill-less, homework-less lives. When it mattered, she'd failed Helena, at least as a listener, but also—by her own standards, at least—as a parent.

That could be a harsh assessment, and her standards weren't exactly the norm. Still, the voice, whatever it wanted to be called, couldn't have been more correct. She acted exactly like all the adults who she swore she'd never be.

"Okay. You're right. I did that, and that's… that's my fault. That's on me, and I'll make it up to her. She and I will have a talk about, well, you, and I'll apologize for not understanding, or realizing what she meant. That doesn't change the fact that you didn't tell me, either."

Tell you what, exactly?

She scowled at the walls. "You know what! The fact that you were talking to my daughter this whole time, having full conversations with her, but never once thought to mention them to me!"

You didn't think to ask. Why should I have assumed you wanted to know?

"Because, maybe, she's my daughter, and I happen to care about what goes on in her life, especially when what's going on is that she's been talking to this person who lives in our walls?"

Oh, stop lying to yourself. That's not why you're angry. You thought I belonged to you, that's why. I spoke to you as a child, and like a child, you clung to this idea that because I was such a big part of your world, I couldn't be part of anyone else's. I may not have children of my own, but I have observed enough to know when one throws a tantrum. Or perhaps this isn't about the fact that I likely saved your life, but the fact that you bought this house, and like your daughter, view I and it synonymously, as if we're one being—as if I really am just The House. Perhaps you assumed that you owned me. Whichever the case, you were wrong, but that possibility never once occurred to you, did it?

Putting her hands over her ears didn't block the voice, They both knew that, but it made her feel better. It provided at least a little distance between her and an unpleasant truth.

Now you cover your ears, pretending you can't hear me. Just. Like. A. Child.

She took her hands away. "Fine! Maybe I didn't know, maybe I didn't even consider, that others could hear you, too, but it's not like I know the rules for this. I grew up thinking you were my guardian angel, and when I came to see this house, had no idea if you'd still be here, or could speak with me again. It didn't seem likely that we could reconnect, and even now, it still seems impossible! Honestly, I'm glad Helena can hear you too, because I'd begun to worry I'd lost it—that maybe you really had always been in my imagination, and the stress of moving, and losing James, and, and everything else, made me have some sort of psychotic break. How can you fault me for all this if you're the spirit, or whatever, and you know so much more than me about this, and didn't once think to say anything?"

I didn't say anything because you had an important lesson to learn. During one of your first days back, you said you moved here, in part, to figure me out, yet you've asked almost nothing about who, or what, I am, or why I'm here. I even told you that others have heard me too, yet you didn't bother to question how that happened, or who heard me, under what circumstances. I gave you all the information you could've needed to make a deduction about Helena on your own, and more than enough to at least inquire further, and yet, you didn't. All you've really asked me is about your mother, and whether I wanted to watch a movie with you and your husband. Should I have rewarded your utter lack of interest and curiosity?

Her pacing slowed as she looked toward the floor, a little hurt, mostly embarrassed. Then she snapped her head up again as she scoured her memories. "Hold on, I *did* ask you about hearing you! Sure, early on, maybe I didn't, but the night I dislocated my shoulder, I asked what changed between those who could hear you and those who couldn't, and what made me special, if I was the first. You didn't reply."

No, you didn't give me a chance to. You got up and started slamming yourself against the door, remember?

Of course she remembered. Her shoulder hadn't finished healing, and the rising pressure brought on by Massachusetts's cold weather made her ache in a deep way that made her worry it would stay painful for the rest of her life. Elijah checked out the door. Perfectly fine.

There'd been nothing wrong with the door.

"I do remember. I remember hearing footsteps, and Helena running past, but when I got out, she was sitting in her room, coloring." Unease stirred her stomach, putting the acid into a boil. "She didn't do that, did she?"

A clatter upstairs almost distracted her, but no, she wouldn't be deterred. If this wasn't just a voice, she had every right to know. They all did. This was something they should've been aware of before buying the place, not that Marcy the Realtor could've known exactly what went on here. At least, she *probably* didn't. Charlotte still didn't know the rules, and all the sudden, her house had fallen oddly quiet.

"Hey, you complained I didn't ask you enough, well, I'm asking now! You creep around, talking to me, talking to *my child,* acting like I didn't deserve answers because I didn't ask the right questions. So, what really happened? Did Helena shut that door, or did you shut it, because I asked something you weren't ready to answer?"

"Babe?" Elijah spoke cautiously from behind her. She turned on her heel, eyes wide, not sure how long he'd been standing there, but absolutely sure he'd been there long enough.

They shared a single moment of couple's silence, the same thought running through their two minds. Every good couple had moments like this, though not necessarily for good reasons. This fell under the 'bad reason' category. For an instant, each found themselves wholly preoccupied by the image of her standing in the basement, talking aloud to someone who wasn't there. Then, as always, their thoughts diverged: hers veered toward defending herself, knowing that her version of reality was correct; his toward protecting Charlotte from herself, as recent events had obviously been a bit more stressful than they'd thought. He didn't think she'd gone insane, no, but everyone has a breaking point, and he needed to make sure she stepped away from it. Far more pressing concerns raced through her mind, as well as the near-certainty that he wouldn't believe a single word of the truth.

"Hi, Honey. How are you?" Charlotte knew this gambit wouldn't accomplish anything, but there remained a one percent chance he'd pretend this hadn't happened.

"Who were you talking to?" His tone made her nostrils flare in agitation. He sounded like all the adults did back when they first learned Charlotte—or "Charlittle" as they liked to call her before puberty and the accompanying growth spurts—had been adopted, on account of her mother's death. That patronizing, over-caring, cyanide-sweet tone made her want to slap him. Just a little. Only because he knew she hated it.

"…Nobody? I didn't say anything."

Oh, so I'm nobody, now?

"Char, I saw you, heard you, whatever. You were talking to someone."

"Rehearsing for a phone call with a difficult client." That had a better chance, or would've, if she'd gone with that first.

He didn't buy it. Crossing his arms, he held eye contact and waited.

"…The House." The truth, or as close as she could come to it, made her shudder. "There's something living in the walls. The same something I heard when Mom died. It's been talking to me."

Elijah gave a slow nod, as if trying to process this, despite it being an obvious act to humor his wife and her clear break from reality. She knew that nod too well. "There's a person living in our walls?"

She sighed. He already thought she was crazy, might as well go the full distance so it all got addressed at once. "It's been there for years, watching through these, I dunno, windows, I guess. The place it lives in is sort of our walls, but more like… like a pocket dimension, or something, a little gap in reality where it can interact with our world while living in another. It doesn't eat or sleep or feel pain, so it says, but this being, The House, if you want to call it that, is definitely alive. It can speak directly into peoples' heads. That's why you don't hear it. But I do. I know how crazy that sounds, but I'm telling the truth. This is… this is the being that saved my life back when I was a little girl."

"Your guardian angel? It's been living here the whole time, waiting for you to come home? That's awfully nice of it." His face took on an inscrutable quality, stone-still and unreadable. Eyes on the floor, peering off into a distant place where he could think more clearly, he suddenly had bags under his eyes, and wrinkles around his mouth. They didn't often talk about how rough life had been for him as a kid, but those wearying years were more visible than usual. Exacerbated, no doubt, by the thought of having to care for yet another person in his life, when she'd been so independent before.

"It's true. I swear, Elijah, I swear it's true." She walked over and put her hands on his shoulders, keeping close, but not so close she might accidentally make him feel threatened. This tightrope-walk of personal space demanded care and attention. "It knows everything that's gone on here, and it can hear us all, and if you don't believe me, ask Helena. She's heard it too."

Dragging your daughter into this?

Elijah, being a good husband, agreed to go talk to Helena. Really, such a conversation could only go two ways: she'd confirm what Charlotte said, and they'd all be ready to talk about this openly, or she'd deny it, and they could discuss the next steps privately. He didn't particularly want to drag their daughter into this, but it'd be the best and fastest way to clarity.

Walking up the stairs elicited a series of groans from the old wood that practically deafened them both. The tension of this situation amplified every little imperfection and nuisance to the point of frustration, and he vowed, before hitting the fifth step, to get some lumber, then tear down and rebuild the steps before Thanksgiving came around. He mentioned the idea to Charlotte, who only shrugged.

Their daughter sat happily watching cartoons on the living room couch. Halloween had fallen on a Friday, after all, so she got to bask in the sugary post-holiday bliss all weekend long. Granted, they rationed the spoils of her trick-or-treating, but after months of hospital food, she didn't mind only getting a few pieces of candy at a time.

Like most children, she could tell her parents had something important to say before they actually spoke. If pressed, Helena couldn't have explained why, but they stood a little straighter than usual, and had a funny look on their face, like they weren't sure what was about to happen. That didn't make sense. Her parents *always* knew what was going on, except for what The House knew. She accepted that. They were partners, her parents and The House, so they didn't need to both know everything. They didn't know the good bedtime stories, and The House couldn't make scrambled eggs.

"Hey, Monkeybutt," her daddy said, crouching down beside her. He didn't say this like he usually did, all funny and happy. It sounded more thoughtful. Far away. The way he sounded when he said she'd have to be in the hospital for a while. "I gotta ask you something."

Your parents have been fighting. They don't want you to worry, but they might hit some rough spots soon. That's okay. Don't worry. As long as you're here, you'll be safe. I'll keep you safe.

"Well, Mommy and I were talking, and… have you noticed anything strange lately?"

Helena thought about this for a second, but everything seemed strange now. James wasn't here. She shrugged.

Her daddy sighed. "I mean, about the house. Does anything seem weird about it to you?"

He's not really asking about me. He's asking about your mom. Your dad is worried about whether or not she's okay. See, people get sick. You know that. But sometimes, it's their brains that get sick, not their bodies. You know how your mom is scared of closed doors? So scared she really hurt herself? That's what he means.

"Like when Mommy hurt her shoulder 'cause she got scared of the door?" The House knew everything that happened inside it. She wasn't surprised that it knew about how that happened.

"Honey, I wasn't scared of the door, that's not how—" But Daddy looked back over his shoulder real quick, and Mommy stopped talking.

"Kinda like that, yeah. You haven't heard anything? Stuff like, maybe, talking?"

"You're talking."

He laughed, just a little. "Yes, I am. I mean someone else talking when you're all alone. Like if you're in your room, coloring, or whenever Mommy and I aren't in the room with you."

You'll never be alone. You have me. But if you tell them you can hear me, they might get jealous and try to keep you away from me. It's okay if you want to tell them the truth. I won't be mad. A little sad if they make you leave, but not mad. You're allowed to be honest.

"Hm…" Helena said, thinking hard. Mommy and Daddy always said the same thing: it's good to be honest. Good kids don't lie, and she liked being good. Telling the truth might make them leave, though. They'd take her away from The House, where she could be safe, not realizing that The House made things better. It could've saved James. It told her so.

"No, not talking. Sometimes I hear Mommy talking, but nobody else."

The room got quiet for a second in that tough way that means something bad happened, but Daddy didn't look at her. He looked down at the floor, then back at Mommy, then at her again.

"But, baby, you said all that stuff, about how The House watches over us. You dressed as The House for Halloween!" Mommy said.

She shrugged. "We dressed up The House to scare people." Helena pointed to the various cheery bats and other spooky decorations in their living room, which didn't come close to the ones outside. "I thought dressing *as* The House would scare people too."

Her parents didn't say anything else. They shared a look for a moment, then Daddy said thank you, and that they were going to talk privately for a moment and walked away. Helena worried they would still split, or leave, or take her away, or that maybe *her* brain got sick and they'd send her back to the hospital.

You think very quickly. Has anyone ever told you how smart you are?

That helped a little.

Really, I mean it. You're a very bright girl. Don't you worry. I'll make sure you're safe. No matter what happens with your parents, you and I will always have each other. Always.

Chapter 12

Elijah laced his work boots and checked that his overnight bag didn't lack any of the necessities: wallet, spare clothes, emergency protein bar and energy drink, a few other odds and ends. All set.

"Eli, please, can't we talk about this?" Charlotte sat in a chair nearby, watching her husband prepare to race out the door. He had places to be, she knew that, but given recent events, couldn't help ask him to stay, if only for a moment.

He shook his head, checking his phone one last time. The Cavanaugh Estate demanded a nearly three hour drive down main thoroughfares, meaning he'd hit traffic, putting him on site in four, maybe five hours if the other drivers really held him up. A single accident would put him there late evening at best, and according to recent calls from Seamus, not to mention other employees, they needed him there within the next five minutes.

Without making eye contact, he tried to reassure his wife, keeping focus on getting his ass out the door. "Listen, I understand what you're saying. I know things have been cra... strange. Hard. Recently, we've hit times that would make anyone completely lose it, so whatever's going on, whatever you're saying, I take it all in stride." An obvious, but necessary, lie. His worldview allowed the possibility of a god, or afterlife, or whatever, but nothing remotely close to what she'd described. They didn't talk about religion or spirituality often because of this. She believed, he didn't. Neither had enough evidence to change the other's mind, so why bother? Such conversation might not lead to a fight, but it'd cause enough tension that bringing it up would never be a good idea.

"I know, I just don't want you to go with our last conversation being a fight. Well, a... whatever you'd call this. Tense situation." Playing the fretful wife didn't suit her. She'd seen enough times, on the news and in her immediate circle of friends, where parting ways on an argument invariably preceded injury, dismemberment, or death. Just a year ago, Marcy O'Donnel and her husband got into a tiff about leaving unwashed dishes in the sink, of all things, and twenty minutes later, she spun out trying to avoid hitting a biker who cut her off. She avoided him successfully, then hit a lamppost. The coroner claimed she died on impact but given how hard her husband cried at the funeral, he may have lied to spare the man further torment. Lies can be comforting, like when Elijah said he didn't think she'd gone insane.

Leaving her with Helena had to be a good sign though, right? He wouldn't do that to his child if he thought his wife had become unstable or dangerous.

"We're not fighting." He finished with his shoes, then zipped his bag. "But here, how's this?" Walking over to her with the sure-footed bootsteps she'd first fallen in love with, back when he barely had aspirations of management, let alone a shot at running a company, Elijah took her hands in his. He knelt down to her level and, finally, looked her in the eyes. "You're a wonderful person, and a wonderful mother. I trust you. I believe in you. Whether you mean all this about the house and every word is true, or whether this is all some… as you'd say, a metaphor, for all we've gone through, and anxiety about what's to come, we'll get through it."

He kissed her forehead. "I need to go help my people up at the estate, and then I'm going to come back, and we're going to make sense of everything. Everything will be perfect again by this time next week. By Thanksgiving, if we decide to be lazy about it. Either way, we're a family. We take care of each other. We'll be okay."

Charlotte knew this to be the truth but didn't believe it. She couldn't. This would all play out like it did the first time around: she'd tell people about the person in the walls, and they'd brush her off as imaginative, then start worrying she'd been damaged by what she'd seen. Talks of her creativity would turn to whispers about PTSD and breaks from reality. Only now, at twenty-eight, she didn't have childhood to fall back on as a defense. People got to thinking she'd lost it this time, and she'd wind up in a nuthouse. God knows she'd spent long enough studying mental illness as a teen, staring at her computer screen well into the night, eyes wide as she whispered to herself, "Oh my god, I have this," and, "Each symptom describes me perfectly." After all that paranoid immersion, it wouldn't be so surprising if her brain finally decided to afflict her with the illnesses that had so terrified her.

Instead of bogging him down with her fears, she kissed him and said, "Okay. I love you."

He kissed her back. As he stood, so did she, and Charlotte walked with him as he descended to the first floor, bid his daughter farewell, then left. Back on the couch, their daughter quietly read a book, oblivious to any lingering tension, her parents' odd behavior earlier that day already forgotten.

You're very trusting.

Helena could hear The House, so Charlotte figured it wouldn't ultimately matter if she spoke to it in front of her daughter, but she couldn't bear the thought of doing so. Walking upstairs to her bedroom once more, she replied, "What do you mean?"

Letting him leave without checking his messages or call history. I've seen couples far more distrusting over far less. People who break into a partner's email because he took a little too long getting home from work, or because she went out to coffee with a friend a few too many times. I once saw a woman make love to her husband in the shower, then cheat on her husband two hours later, throwing herself at a well-chiseled lover like he was the last glass of water on a barren earth. Some people are insatiable. Some people can't be trusted. If your husband isn't either of those two, then perhaps you really do have something special.

Obviously, she trusted him. Any good relationship is built on trust, and not just the romantic ones. Friends, family, roommates, even friends with benefits, all demanded certain—but different—levels of trust. If she didn't trust Elijah, she wouldn't have married him.

"Of course he is. Of course we do, I mean. Have something special. There's not a chance in the world he'd cheat on me. He's not the type, and besides, his parents would smack him silly if they found out he so much as tried to have an affair."

Wasn't talking about sleeping around, but sure, that's good too.

It didn't explain further. The House—she hated calling it that, but at this point, why not?—fell silent, and the silence held no tension, no pregnant pause as the speaker geared up to deliver a more difficult point. She'd grown used to such overbearing wordlessness in the hospital, but this one instance, this quip that demanded *she* be the one to speak, goading her curiosity until it killed her, felt worse. Being drawn into conversation was oddly similar to being a fly lured toward a bug zapper.

"Okay, what do you mean by that?" She couldn't simply let the comment go.

What I mean is, he seemed very sure that you're unwell, and all the sudden, he has to leave immediately? The timing seems a bit too convenient. Didn't you used to see a therapist?

"Yes, but not for—"

Then what are the odds he's gone to consult with the good doctor about your recent turn for the worse? Getting an expert opinion on how to best approach the situation without setting you off, keeping his daughter as safe as possible? After all, him rushing off for work, he knew you'd be okay with that, as you were. How would you have reacted if he said he had to leave for any other reason? Forgot something at the store, or had to visit his parents, for example?

If he'd suddenly dashed off into the afternoon with a flimsy excuse right after they had an almost-fight, wherein he seemed to think she'd had a psychotic episode? She had to admit an obvious truth. "…I wouldn't have handled it very well." Her hands clenched, wringing each other like old towels. "I'd have thought he just wanted out and came up with some bad excuse to get away."

The House didn't say anything, simply left her to stew in her own thoughts, which had never been a great idea. "He's done that before, you know. Always has. Our fourth date, I told him about being adopted, and five minutes later, he looked at his wrist and said, 'Oh, crap, I forgot, I promised Dad I'd help him move some furniture. Getting up there, he can't do it all on his own anymore.' I tried being okay with it, since that was only date four, but I realized an hour after he drove off that he hadn't been wearing a watch. Idiot literally just looked at his bare wrist, gave the first bad excuse he could think of, and bailed, because my being adopted was too intense. He called the next day to apologize. I almost didn't answer." She began pacing. Every conversation with The House felt like being on the phone, talking endlessly into a receiver with no actual person to lay eyes on.

Yet, you went out again afterward. Why, if he acted so callously?

Charlotte bit her lip, unable to stop thinking about where he really went, or why. What if officers came busting down the front door to take her daughter away? Well, Elijah would be with them, so they probably would just use the key rather than destroy their property, but either way, not a great formative experience for their child.

"The way he told it, it came out sweet. Eli asked if we could meet up, and he explained how family was all he'd had, for so long, and it scared him to think of a life where he didn't have the people he loved. He wasn't sure how to connect with me, if he'd say the wrong thing, or if I'd be able to be part of a new family some day. Apparently, his father set him straight. Sat him down and asked him, plain and simple, if I'd grown up in a box, or with a foster family. He already knew about my new parents, my siblings, all that, so Eli explained and..." Charlotte smiled a little, laughing at the idea. "And his dad smacked him in the back of the head. 'Family's what you make of it, so even if she's not raised by blood, she's still got parents, dummy.'" Her impression of a grizzled old man sounded more at home on a children's cartoon than an actual person, but it got the point across.

Sounds like you're fond of his family, as well as your own.

Tapping her fingers against her thighs, Charlotte slowed, then turned to her best approximation of which wall the being currently lurked inside. "Yeah. I am. Family's what you make of it, and when I married him, his parents became my family too. In fact, I think that's the moment I realized I could love Elijah. Not the moment I *did,* just that I *could,* because his family... they all felt like people I'd be proud to call my relatives."

Makes sense that you take that stance. That you're willing to call family anyone who keeps you close and treats you well. You mention that your father has never reappeared, but your mother's case is still open. So, he's not in prison—presumably—but he abandoned you, and never returned. Even as an adult, you struggle to fill the void left by his departure.

Those few sentences knocked the air from her. Her therapists had all said roughly the same exact thing. She swallowed the sudden knot building in her throat. "Why would you bring that up?"

It seemed relevant. All this talk of family, but in all our conversations, you've never dwelled on him, nor asked about him. Nor your mother, actually. You've asked how she died, but never expressed interest in further detail. It's surprising.

"I thought you hadn't been here long before they... left?"

I hadn't. Only... oh, it's been so long, now. Five days, I think. Yes. Five, I'd been here, crawling through the gaps between the walls, when your mother met her untimely end, scaring your father out of your life forever.

"Five days. Hardly seems long enough to get to know them." Charlotte crossed her arms, no longer pacing, and leaned her back against the wall, glaring across the room at where she presumed the being to be.

Didn't say I knew them well, just enough. That would seem to be a fairly important length of time either way, wouldn't it? Even if it's only a glimpse, I can offer you a window into their lives. I can offer you an understanding of the only family you didn't get to choose.

Her stomach twisted. This didn't seem right. Even if it told the truth, why unbury the dead? What good would it serve her to ask? "I'm fine, thanks."

You move back here to resolve all the loose ends of your mother's death, and—

"And I said I'm fine. Thanks."

Am I sensing hostility?

"You're sensing that I'm not interested in learning who they were, because I can't miss what I don't remember. Why would you want to dredge up those memories?"

This time, the silence weighed heavily all around her, crushing down with its own terrible gravity. She'd struck a nerve, she could tell, and maybe this being didn't feel physical pain, but the tension screamed emotional torment. "…I think you like to dwell on the lives of the people who lived here because it's all you've got. You're stuck in there, and you have no idea how to get out, and it infuriates you that we all walk around the rooms, free to do as we want."

I have ideas.

"Sure you do. That's why you spend all day talking to a five-year-old or bugging me about my marriage. You've got no plans, no ideas, no hope."

Hope is for the weak who don't know how to overcome their situation. I won't be in here much longer, I can promise you that, as I've promised Helena the same.

She laughed, trying to hide her mounting fear. What the hell did that mean, he wouldn't be here much longer? And why was this thing making promises to her daughter? "Sure you won't. Twenty-five years in there, and now you expect me to believe that something's suddenly changed? Face it: you're never going to get out, and you're powerless to even try."

A massive force slammed into the wall behind her, sending her sprawling to the floor as the lights flickered. The house rocked with the impact of a cannon ball, her back pulsing to broadcast a coming bruise, but she barely noticed, her attention drawn instead to a slight crack now running along the wall. It radiated outward from a single tight, fist-sized impact point where her dislocated shoulder had rested. Downstairs, Helena yelped, and Charlotte's instinct was to run to her, but she stopped herself. If The House had focused on her, running to her daughter would only put the girl in its sights.

Do not dare to presume what I can do.

Her door slammed shut, lock clicking into place as the flickering lights went out.

Chapter 13

Charlotte washed the dishes as loudly as she could, but didn't speak.

The House kept her locked in the bedroom for hours. She banged, she yelled, she called for Helena, but got nowhere. Even when she released the lock, the door stayed sealed. When it finally let her go, Helena sat happily on the couch, glancing over with the smug look every child gets when she realizes her parents aren't all-powerful.

Since then, Charlotte vacuumed the living room twice to pretend she couldn't hear Helena talking upstairs, then put on the TV so she could fold laundry in peace. The news broadcasted a story she only half-heard about an incident at a local high school, where a boy was found severely injured in a custodial supply room, but authorities couldn't determine how he sustained the injuries, or how he'd gotten locked inside. She didn't listen. A person can only care so much about so many things, and at that moment, she fought the urge to think about the only person she cared about.

Well, she cared about two people, but only one warranted attention, and she couldn't do a damn thing about that. She couldn't talk to Helena about The House because, where could they possibly talk? Every surface served as an eye, an ear, an arm. If they came close at all, maybe by blasting the TV and talking directly into each other's ears, it would still know they were plotting something. If they spoke directly, without regard for it listening, she had no idea what it might do. Even texting seemed like a bad idea. It could always be watching.

She had to try though. Once the idea crossed her mind, it wouldn't leave, and hearing her kid upstairs talking to it only spurred her on. The throbbing ache of her nearly re-sprained shoulder helped, too.

Glancing around, as if that might help, she pulled up Elijah's contact info in her messenger app. **Honey, something bad happened. I really pissed off the house. We need to leave. Bring all your tools and, I don't know, cut the front door off or something.**

Charlotte hit send, bit her lip, and decided to clarify: **It won't let us leave.**

When she'd been three, it helped her escape. Now, that same front door wouldn't open, and this time, The House kept it shut. It wasn't locked. It just wouldn't open. The windows wouldn't open either. It didn't bother speaking or warning her not to resist. It knew she couldn't.

Helena must have left a tissue in her pocket, because a thousand scraps of white clung to every possible corner of the laundry. She must've had a hundred talks with her about doing that, but today wouldn't be number one-oh-one. Oh no. Not while she kept The House busy. Talking to her now would mean talking to it, too, and all the paper-besotted pants in the world wouldn't convince her to talk to it.

Her phone chirped, and in her haste to pick it up, she knocked it into the couch cushions. Swearing at herself under her breath, she shoved her arm in as deep as she could, fumbling for that stupid rectangle of hard plastic as pointy bits scraped at her hand. For a moment, she worried these little nicks were The House's claws, raking at her flesh. She shook her head to dispel the notion. She may never have seen it before, but she knew its claws wouldn't be that small. This fact reassured her for the present, shoving her worry to the future.

By the time she latched onto the phone, her hand felt like it had been through a cactus patch. Yanking hard, Charlotte freed it, her hand covered in chicken scratches, chest heaving, consciousness only dimly aware of how truly anxious she'd become. This didn't merit a shrink or dose. This time, she had every right to feel a little worked up, and she may not have been a violent person, but if even one person told her it wasn't a big deal, she'd break their god damn nose.

No signal.

"No," she whispered, only half caring if it heard, because it likely jammed the signal, so it probably already knew. "No way. No, you fucking house."

Dropping her head into her hands, she tried not to think about The House, or the present, or anything about her immediate reality. The news had switched over to yet another missing person's story. Four pairs of pants and a few t-shirts still needed folding. Upstairs, a high-pitched giggle resounded from Helena's bedroom.

Her mom died barely twenty feet from where she sat. What would she have done? Would her being alive have changed anything? All the stories of her childhood featured some kind of magical parent figure: Cinderella's Fairy Godmother, Glinda the Good Witch, the three fairies watching over Aurora in Sleeping Beauty, Mufasa—even as a ghost—caring for Simba. Mary Poppins counted, too, and so did Tinkerbell, depending on how you viewed her relationship with Peter Pan.

Charlotte tried to cling to these ideas, that a good, gifted, morally upstanding person would hop into her life and fix everything, or at least teach her how to fix things herself. That never happened, and probably for good reason. That reason wasn't a lack of magic in the world. It was becoming increasingly apparent that the world, perhaps, had too much of the unexplained.

The reason was that those magical beings only offered their support when the protagonist hit rock bottom. Simba's father died. Aurora slipped into a coma. Dorothy wound up thousands of miles from home in a foreign land. Cinderella had her step-family, with no hope of escape.

No hope of escape.

Those were the magic words. The incantation a child's heart had to scream in order for those beings to come assist. When she watched her mother die, and her father run out the front door, the ache in her chest became a beacon that woke this house, but she did one thing that no fairy tale protagonist dared: she left the magic behind. Now, it had become powerful, and angry at her betrayal. Now, it answered her daughter's call instead.

She'd invited it into her life, then moved here to get it back when she thought her son's death would be too much for her to bear. She hadn't thought twice about the fact that she was an adult now. Magic didn't work for adults. Fairies, spirits, imps, whatever someone might call this thing in her house, aren't here to help those who should be able to help themselves. They only protect the innocent.

Maybe The House was right. She had, after all, moved here with the exact intention it so easily read: Charlotte remembered this being in the walls, and wanted it all to herself. It made up a part of her childhood she thought she deserved total ownership of, this little scrap of validation that no, she had never simply been an imaginative child, that there really had been someone here. Someone only she could hear, and god, she'd left it all alone, for so, so long.

How could she fault it for being angry? Prisoners who wind up doing just a week in solitary emerge frightful and traumatized. Those who spend longer in isolation, those who remain in that lonely dark for weeks or months on end, often go insane. It's hard to spend that much time with yourself and not become someone else entirely. It's a reverse exposure therapy. Most times, being saturated in the negative trigger cures you—a person afraid of snakes just gets in a pit of snakes until they aren't afraid anymore. But yourself? If you stew in your own darkness for long enough, you don't become the light. Survival means burrowing deeper into the subconscious and making a nest deep in the blackest core of your being, where light has never had any hope of reaching.

So many people told her she was crazy. Would-be foster parents. Fellow children. Child therapists. It probably wasn't professional to say, "You're insane," but she'd heard it enough to almost believe it. More than feeling crazy, she'd only ever felt alone. But, being alone long enough makes you feel pretty crazy.

Leaving the unfolded laundry in the basket, Charlotte walked into the kitchen, almost knocked on the wall, but put her back to it, sliding to the floor. She huddled in the corner of the room, resting her head on the adjacent wall, knees to her chest, and raised her hand. Knocking twice on the wall behind her led to a sudden hush from upstairs.

Then, as always, the walls began to creak, the floors groaning as an impossible, yet still oddly human being crawled along the gaps between surfaces. It settled in the plaster nearby, where she felt its eyes on her, tense but reserving judgement.

Yes?

"I'm sorry," Charlotte whispered from far away. The words didn't feel like her own, though part of her still meant them. Part of them had to, or she wouldn't be saying them. "It's just… I lost one child already. I've been so scared for Helena, that when I learned you could talk to her, all I could think about was how I started talking to you. If something happened to her, that's it. That'd be all I could take. So… sorry. Being passionate doesn't give me a right to be cruel."

Apology accepted. I understand why you got so emotional. You feel like you're the only person Helena should ever need. Between not having me to yourself, and not having her to yourself, you felt cut out, so you threw a selfish little tantrum. Believe me. I understand.

She nodded against the plaster, a tear rolling down her cheek. "My little girl."

It's the same reason you take her on all those little excursions, but Elijah only gets a few fleeting moments of Daddy-Daughter time. You've only had yourself, so you only trust yourself. That lone wolf mentality makes people selfish. You'll learn to share her with the world, though. Every parent does. It's part of your child growing up. You're not the first parent to live here, and I've learned a lot from watching other families. Maybe you could learn how to be a real parent from me, if you're not busy pretending to know everything.

"You wouldn't mind?" Her stomach knotted at the thought, but she'd followed her instincts before, and it led to a hole in the wall with the doors sealed shut. Maybe now was the time to put a little faith in this being. "I just want her to grow up healthy and happy. That's all."

Don't worry, Charlotte. She will. I'll make sure of it.

Chapter 14

By the time Elijah came back, their home settled into an unusual quietude. No one really spoke. Helena nodded sleepily on the couch, head bobbing out of sync with the theme song to yet another inane children's program. Charlotte spoke with The House sporadically throughout the afternoon, asking its thoughts on life, on her family, on anything it felt like sharing, but neither of them felt it a good idea to return to the subject that catalyzed their fight: moving out. It, from the walls, or them, from the building. Either one, really, would've risked setting something off.

Her husband looked more haggard than usual. Typically, after nights away for various projects, he'd get back unshaved, dark-eyed, with that tired, self-assured smile, the kind that says, "Baby, you got no idea how tired I am, and damn if every second wasn't worth it." Early on, those trips away worried her. Some of her friends had lovers take 'work trips' to the Hyatt one town over to spend a few hours with a lover, call girl, escort, or whatever name the partner cooked up to rationalize the affair. This hadn't been limited to male-female relationships, either. Ray spent the last month of his engagement to Phillip screwing a woman from work because "he still wasn't sure," and when Lana came down with chlamydia for the third time, Kelsey owned up to having a free for all with every hooker she laid eyes on.

Charlotte felt certain Elijah would one day have some dark confession of his own, but that day never came. This last time, she worried maybe he finally would, had spent their first night apart since the wedding day tossing fitfully, sure to hell and back again that between James, moving, and catching her talking out loud to "no one," he'd go for a little horizontal refreshment with any palette cleanser that could fog a mirror. Assuming, of course, that he had no intention of returning with police or child services to take their daughter away.

None of that happened. He walked in the door slowly, eyes so deep in his skull they could've been set by a well digger. The normally springy, boyish hair she loved to run her hands through had fallen flat, tousled by a cold wind. He dropped his overnight bag by the door. She almost asked why he did that, since he was such a stickler for keeping things neat, and she had just vacuumed anyway. When she made eye contact, she decided not to. His gaze stayed locked on something far off, so she just put a hand on his shoulder and guided him to the kitchen, past their almost-dozing daughter.

"What's going on?" she whispered.

He took a seat at the table, shaking his head. The hands that gripped his chair were blistered raw with first degree burns, and minor scratches ran along his arms. "Seamus is dead."

"Jesus." Charlotte slid another chair out and sat next to him, taking his hands in hers to assess the damage. If he felt any pain, he didn't say so. "What happened up there?"

His eyes glazed over again. She'd taken a CPR course once and knew well enough to see that he was in shock. Mentally berating whoever had let him drive, she hopped up, got him water and half a leftover turkey club, then rejoined him. He took hold of the cup but didn't drink.

"I think I owe you an apology." Outside, the sun began to set, but gave no trace of the usual colorful sky. They skipped the light show and went straight to a moonless dark. "I've never... never believed in anything. Dad did, Mom did, some of my brothers and sisters did, sometimes, but me, no. Didn't see how anything could really be out there, you know? Growing up the way I did, house to house, paycheck to paycheck, listening to kids make fun of me at school 'cause none of us had showered in days, but having to go anyway or I wouldn't eat... There's no room in a life like that for gods or devils or anything but how shitty people could be."

He trailed off, but his eyes focused in, just a little. They drank in the room like two beggars, dying of thirst in a desert, while surrounded by people with canteens. Water everywhere, not a single drop to drink.

"Yesterday, though. Yesterday." Blisters trembled on his red skin as his hands shook. "Remember when he—Seamus—came by, how he thought we could do renovations, impress the owners, and flip the place?" Charlotte nodded. "We're not supposed to modify anything because the owner's not a person, it's a trust. The trust oversees the estate, and some other factors relating to the Cavanaugh family. We answer to them, and when we talked about the modification clauses, I thought they were just insistent. But I think they were afraid."

Elijah shook harder than she'd seen any grown man shake before. From the couch came light snoring, so rather than wake her daughter to ensure she'd go to bed on time, Charlotte put a hand to her husband's whiskery jawline. "Whatever happened, it's going to be okay. Like you said, we're family. We'll get through it."

For whatever that was worth, it helped enough to get his story going again. "There are rumors about that place. About someone still living there—someone not exactly human. Obviously, I brushed it off. The more superstitious folks took their little precautions. Seamus, blowhard that he is—was—didn't give a damn. Four of us were upstairs in a guest bedroom on the third floor when he started marking up the wall. Said he wanted to knock it out, surprise the trust, maybe convince them to flip it, let us sell for a profit. Room started getting dark. I thought the lights were giving out, or he kept kicking up dust, but then I smelled it. Smoke."

He swallowed hard, looking out the sliding glass doors to the back. "Before I could say anything, he started up the saw and it just… blew. Never saw one malfunction like that before. Sent the blade right back into his chest, blasted his hand off, set him on fire. Scrap metal lodged in one of his eye sockets. Everything that could possibly happen to him did. Every fucking possible thing."

"Holy shit, babe." They could both get a pass on the no-swearing rule tonight.

"Not even sure how he died. Burning? Shock? Bleeding out? God, I hope that miserable bastard croaked the second it all went to shit. Thing is, though, all that burning smell, the ash cloud, it started up when we didn't have anything on. When it all went south, I could swear I saw a smoggy gray hand, ready to tear it up from inside."

Elijah got up, shaking his head hard, his normally straight-backed but easy-going posture hunched, frantic, scrabbling for mental purchase in an ideological avalanche. He stepped out of his work boots, having just enough presence of mind to pace without waking his daughter. Nostrils flaring, he sucked in air like each breath might be his last.

"That thing, Char? They call it The Smoke Siren. The One Who Burns. That works two ways, you know—being on fire, and being the one to start the fire." He took a few desperate, shaking lung fulls. "I think a demon killed Seamus."

She knew she should approach him, or reassure him, or lay her hands on his shoulders, or do some basic thing to remind him that life goes on and it would all be okay, but she couldn't. This Eli didn't feel like her husband. Half the reason she fell in love with him was the fact that he, the non-believer, the rational skeptical cynic in all things, would talk her down from her lofty ideas. Knowing they might both be the weird, cryptid-hunting, lore-believing partner in their coupling made her nervous.

Yet, he'd humored all her middle-of-the-road insanity. He stood by her through so much already, and never once doubted her stories about the presence she heard as a child. Even before he left for this night away, if she looked through the veil of her anxieties, she knew he was at least fifty percent sincere about taking her seriously. Maybe he didn't entirely believe her, but he loved her enough to try. She loved him enough to do the same.

Approaching him slow, like she might approach a wounded animal—because that, she realized, is exactly what he was—she took his blistered hands again and raised them to her lips. She kissed his charred knuckles, keeping her eyes on his, making sure he maintained eye contact. If they wanted to talk about this, he'd have to stay here, not there.

"That must've been horrifying to see. I'm really sorry. For him, and for you."

He nodded. "I never want to see that again."

"The odds of that exact scene happening twice are pretty low."

She said it before she could stop herself and bit her tongue in the silent seconds after. To her overwhelming relief, a grin split his face. He started with a chuckle, soon progressing to a hearty laugh, burying his face in her neck to avoid waking Helena. Charlotte laughed too, letting go of his hands to hug him. Laughing in a moment like that could feel terrible, but humor, no matter how subtle, keeps people grounded.

Alternatively, she once heard it said that thinking is the enemy of comedy, so if she could keep him entertained, he wouldn't dwell on Seamus. All things considered, the prospect of turning their life into a gag reel seemed pretty low.

The happy couple, together again.

Charlotte ignored The House, for now. It could wait. So many things could wait, so long as they had laughter, and each other. Except dinner.

"It's getting late, and it's been a long few days. Chinese?" Charlotte asked.

He kissed her. It wasn't the same, though. His lips used to meet hers with warmth and tenderness. Now, they almost sealed themselves to hers, firm and desperate, clinging to them as a life raft in waters he hadn't realized were vast, cold, and very, very dark.

Chapter 15

Charlotte didn't know how to bring up The House. She didn't have time to. Thanksgiving Day loomed just a week off, and that Thursday glowed on the calendar they'd hung in the kitchen, those two words written in the same heavy font as Black Friday. They'd sent out invites over a month ago; canceling now would make them look terrible, but something had to be done. How were they supposed to cook a whole Thanksgiving Dinner, given their current state of affairs?

"All I'm saying is that we could ask people to bring sides." Elijah's head and heart both went to the right places, but how utterly gauche. Ask both their families to put in work just to, what, earn the right to show up? That didn't even cover how embarrassing it would be for everyone if two people made the same dish, and heaven forbid one of the two be clearly better than the other. That's the sort of shame that people die from, provided they don't have a supernatural being living in their walls to give them a little perspective.

"We could ask them to bring sides, yes, or we could ask your brother to bring one of his hunting rifles and put us out of our misery. People ask why we sent out invites, then made them do all the work."

"That cheapskate would probably make us pay for the bullets, so let's find another solution." He grinned, but not like he used to. Elijah hadn't been there to watch James pass. He'd had work to do, and they couldn't both shirk their responsibilities. Her freelance income had almost dried up. Even as the boss, he could only afford so many sick days before his middle management staged a coup. It killed him, metaphorically, to have not been there, but now that he'd actually witnessed someone die—and so horribly, at that—it seemed this was killing him literally. The last time he'd looked this pale, he'd been diagnosed with strep throat, pneumonia, and tonsillitis at the hospital, after passing out mid-shift down at the Haverford Mills Road site.

They had important matters to discuss that weren't about food. She didn't know how to bring them up in any kind of safe or rational way. Looking at him, Charlotte couldn't put any extra burden on him, or bear the thought of him walking out again. It felt like he'd be leaving to curl up in a storm drain and wait for death to come.

Fortunately, she didn't have to do anything.

"Charlotte?" He spoke up from behind her while she made a frittata. Breakfast had been light. Why not treat everyone?

"Yes?" After a moment of no response, she looked back to see him struggling to say something. "Cat got your tongue?" They both hated cats, but the expression made her chuckle, thinking of a cat with its paws shoved into someone's mouth.

He drummed his fingers on the counter, then looked at the ceiling, the walls, the ceiling again, and turned back to her. "Tell me about The House." This time, the words didn't take on a tone of condescension. Just worry. Curiosity. Maybe fear.

Turning her back to the food, she waded in slowly. "Well, like you know, when I was a girl, and… and mom died, I started hearing this voice. It came from the walls, and it helped guide me on how to get out. When we came back to look at this property, I heard it again. All this time, it's been here, watching. Listening. Waiting, I guess. It's talked to Helena, too."

Elijah gave no indication of actually hearing her, but the way they sank into the silence after, he clearly had a lot to think about. Helena had homework to do, so she sat up in her room, writing the alphabet ad nauseum, coloring, and doing all the menial little tasks the school made kids do to prepare them for the spine-crushing workload they'd face as teenagers. In the meanwhile, she could enjoy school while she still thought it just meant singing songs and eating snacks. None of the walls creaked, nor floors groaned, but Charlotte could tell The House watched them closely.

"How do you feel about it? About this… spirit, being, creature, whatever it is?" He trekked the conversation carefully, taking slow steps up loose stones on a near-straight drop back down the mountain of their lives, not sure either of them could survive the fall.

Food demanded at least some attention, so she continued prepping to ensure nothing would burn or generally fall to pieces, but her heart wasn't in it anymore. "I… I'm not sure. I feel bad for it, I think. This being, The House, I guess, has been here for twenty-five years, living in isolation. I'm not sure why I can hear it, or Helena, but all that time spent with no one to talk to, but being able to see people come and go, had to be hard. I would've gone insane. Most people would've. That's the main reason I feel like it isn't human. If it were, it would be totally crazy by this point."

"And you like it being here? Like being in a house like this?"

"I do. It's interesting. Unique. Fun. We get along, most times, so why not?" She was pretty sure she told the truth, but still appreciated having her back to him. Made the conversation easier.

"Most times?"

She paused, mid-egg crack. It began leaking onto the counter, but she didn't budge. By the time she did, she'd made a mess of the counter. "Yeah. Most times."

"That's where the hole upstairs came from, huh? The damage to the bedroom wall?"

"…I did that. I was upset by our conversation and, uh, punched the wall."

He snorted. "Babe, I love you, but you're a fuckin' terrible liar. Sorry, language, but still. You dislocated your shoulder opening a door, and I've watched you swerve to avoid hitting roadkill. No way in hell did you punch a wall, let alone that hard."

Charlotte almost tried to argue, but he cut her off. "Besides, I work in reconstruction. I'm no detective or whatever but assessing damage to a building is kinda my thing. That wall got busted from the inside."

She let her eyes drift shut. "So you don't think I'm crazy anymore?"

Two strong arms wrapped around her. For a fleeting second, she thought he might offer words of comfort. Instead, he whispered, "I hear it too."

Chapter 16

They hadn't spent enough time together as a family lately. Since they moved in, really. James's death really threw them out of sync. Every dinner together left an empty seat; every movie night, an open spot on the couch. You can't fill the void left by a lost child, but you can't ignore it, either. That absence, like space itself, is a cold vacuum that suffocates whatever gets lost inside it, and only the wisp-thin atmosphere of love for her remaining family kept Charlotte from dying in that void.

She'd been a little more selfish than she wanted to admit. Selfishness is natural, during mourning and otherwise. It's part of what makes people human. It's part of why people are inherently flawed. The need to stroke and feed their ego is what's provided humankind with the evolutionary advantage to adapt and overcome its obstacles. It also provided the vicious streak that drove humans to kill off any threat to cross its path, even when that threat was sleeping, running away, or, all too often, another group of humans.

This family meeting hardly seemed like the optimal way to squeeze in more family activity, but what else could she do? It was time they talked about The House for real. They couldn't have some huge unspoken secret hanging over them during Thanksgiving. As such, they'd set up a pillow fort in the living room. It gave the illusion of security, where they'd be safe from prying eyes, though she knew The House could creep to the floors just beneath them. Maybe the pillows would muffle their voices, giving them a real chance to talk.

They couldn't exactly leave. Helena refused to and would scream loud enough for the neighbors to come knocking if they tried to take her against her will. The House let Elijah leave, as long as he left his phone. The doors would slam tight once he left, keeping Charlotte inside.

She trusted this being, as much as she could bring herself to trust anyone but wasn't sure if she liked herself for trusting it. It kept trying to control them, and she rationalized this by insisting they hurt it first, but had they?

Helena lied to them about it. That marked the first time she'd told a real lie. Children always make stories up to test boundaries—"Yes, I brushed my teeth," "I don't have homework today," "I've only been watching for ten minutes!" "I ate all my broccoli"—but telling her an outright false story about a situation like this merited a real talk.

"Hey, Monkeybutt," Elijah said, after an hour or so of reading ghost stories by flashlight, as if it wasn't three in the afternoon. He kept his voice low, just in case. "Mommy and I have a question for you."

Like all children, she had an innate sense of when life had taken a sharp left turn toward trouble. When she spoke, her lips stayed close together, her words clipped. "Okay, Daddy."

"Well, remember when we asked about the house, and if you'd noticed strange stuff?"

She nodded.

"Remember when you said you hadn't noticed anything, but said it was weird that Mommy got scared of the door? Or how the only talking you heard was Mommy?" His gaze flicked toward Charlotte. Helena looked up at her, then down at a pillow she clung to, a little pink square about the size of her torso.

"Now, it's okay. Don't worry. We're not gonna be mad. But we don't think you told us the truth back there," Charlotte added. Solidarity mattered a lot in parenting. If she sat passively by, it'd change their whole dynamic.

"I didn't lie." Her tiny, pained murmur hurt to hear.

"Well, Mommy and Daddy both hear The House too," Eli said. Helena's head snapped up, attention fixed behind watery eyes. "And I think maybe it told you not to tell us about it because it didn't think I'd understand."

"I also think The House shut my door. I'm really sorry I yelled at you for that," Charlotte said, "but The House didn't tell me it could do that. You didn't tell me either."

Helena looked back at her little pillow. "I didn't know."

"That's okay. None of us did."

"Did The House tell you to lie to us?"

Their daughter shrugged, so they pressed further. She nodded.

They exchanged a glance and nodded to each other.

"Well, we've been talking. Maybe this wasn't the best decision."

Helena stopped playing with her pillow. Her head slowly tilted back up, making steady contact with now-dry eyes, pupils blown out a bit too large to blame solely on their slightly dark pillow fort. "What do you mean?"

"We mean…" Charlotte said, taking a slow breath. "Maybe we should move again. To a smaller place, and a better neighborhood, where—"

"No!" Helena jumped up, knocking the blanket and pillows away. Her shriek bounced off the walls, practically echoing, definitely hurting their eardrums. "The House said you would do this! The House said you would take me away! That's why I didn't tell you!"

If it hadn't heard them before, the being in the walls definitely heard them now. "Helena, honey, stop yelling," Elijah said.

"No. The House is my friend, and I love it, and you're being mean and taking me away when we should have come here sooner! The House could have saved James." She balled her little fists and shook herself red.

Choking back a lump in her throat, Charlotte said, "Sweetie, he was sick. Even if we had lived here, he died in the hospital, not here. The House couldn't have saved him."

"You didn't want him around! Just like you don't want me!" Her shriek hit a glass-shatter pitch, then dropped back down to strained, but barely controlled, anger. "You're mean, and you work and all you care about is if I'm coloring or reading and you not spending time with me, but the house tells me bedtime stories, and it doesn't ignore me or tell me to go watch TV to talk to the grown-ups! That's why I love The House and not you!"

Charlotte and Elijah exchanged a nod. They'd prepared for this, just in case, lovingly titled 'Operation: Who Cares About Thanksgiving.'

Elijah wrapped Helena in his arms and hoisted her up, marching toward the door. "The House doesn't mean what it says. We're going to spend some time away from it."

"No, no, no!" She squirmed. "House! Help!"

The deadbolt snapped into place. Then the windows slammed shut, one by one, but way too fast for an average-sized person. If it really did just use two hands to do all this, the way the panes all rushed down almost simultaneously confirmed her suspicions about its unnaturally long reach. She didn't have to test the windows though. They'd been sealed inside.

Helena bit Elijah hard on the forearm. He cried out, dropping her, putting pressure on the wound as she scurried away to the couch, mouth stained red. They didn't get a chance to move. A familiar cannonball blast rocked the house, the living room floors splintering, followed by another three bangs that broke entire boards and made her almost entirely certain of their imminent plummet to the basement. She looked at Elijah, and when The House spoke, she knew from his face that they both heard it.

Where do you think you're taking my daughter?

Chapter 17

"**M**y daughter?" Charlotte repeated, first out of shock, then again out of anger. "My daughter? What—who—Helena is my child, not yours!"

The child has the right to be raised by the parent of her choosing. You've been neglectful, and selfish, and she hasn't seemed very fond of the fact that you place all your wants above hers.

If she hadn't been living here, she would've thought she'd gone insane. Part of her hoped everyone else was right, that she just imagined all this, that watching her mother die so young knocked a couple screws loose, leaving them to rattle around in her skull, creating some kind of house-demon hybrid. Why not, right? She'd rationalized Helena's comments as a child needing a friend, or guardian. Every time the kid brought up the fact that The House watched over them, she told herself this was just a little girl in need of an imaginary friend after the horrible, untimely death of her twin brother. It wouldn't be such a huge leap to assume that she did the same thing and believing in this spirit all these years had left a fault line in her brain, waiting to shift, to tear her consciousness down to the ground at the slightest provocation. Such a theory would explain why she felt so compelled to return only after losing her boy.

All this might've made sense, and she might even have taken comfort in the idea that she'd totally lost her mind, if not for Elijah's look of abject terror. Poor guy. The rationalist, the logical one, the man she loved for his ability to see reason even in the most unreasonable situations, watched one of his coworkers die, then had to come back and face the fact that a sentient house was trying to raise his daughter.

Charlotte almost spoke, then didn't, ideas too busy running through her mind to dare cross her tongue. The realtor kept trying to talk about death disclosures, but she'd waved her off. She'd been too busy not wanting to hear about her mother to listen closely. The woman hadn't said disclosure, singular. She'd said disclosures. Plural.

Already knowing the answer, she turned to her daughter. "Helena, sweetie… what are The House's bedtime stories about?"

The girl, still angry, her lips set in a resolute pout, looked around, confused. "They're about all the people who used to live here."

She swallowed back the apprehension occluding her throat. "Those are scary stories, right? Like ghost stories. The kind we tell in our pillow forts. Has The

House been telling stories about how all those people died?"

Helena nodded, exuberance temporarily overshadowing her confusion. "The House knows everything. It sees all the stuff people do inside it. ...But how did you know?"

Charlotte and Elijah exchanged the long, slow eye contact of two people that know each other well enough to border on telepathy. He may not have fully understood the details, but he didn't have to. He got the message. Charlotte and her mother. Helena and James. Elijah and Seamus. The pattern couldn't be much clearer.

"Death. It's death. That's how people hear you. They only know you're here if they've watched someone die. All the people who die here, that just gives you more power. More control. That's why you can seal the doors now, isn't it?" The House didn't reply, but she knew damn well she was right, so she spun, looking to every wall, to the ceiling, demanding an answer with her eyes. "When I first heard you, you couldn't do anything! I had to call 9-1-1 because there was no chance of either of us opening the door. Now you—you... how many? How many have you killed?"

The walls didn't creak, and the floors didn't groan, but she knew it was listening. Even if it didn't talk back, it sure as hell heard her, not that she cared anymore. Getting out of that house now fell into all ten slots of her top priority list, so she stepped forward, intending to cross the broken boards and grab Helena. Even if they couldn't get out, it would make her feel a little better, using her body, her heartbeat, to protect and calm the child, as she had once before. Charlotte didn't get that far. After just one step, all the floors gave way, for both her and Elijah, sending them down into the basement with a single cry.

Now Helena's smug superiority had faded. She didn't know the word 'killed,' but she'd only heard Mommy or Daddy this upset once before, and knew it had to be bad. They only sounded like this when James stopped being alive. She did know the words 'die' and 'death,' and Mommy might not have made much sense, but she still felt wrong. Watching Mommy and Daddy disappear into the basement like that felt the same as the time she stole James's crayons. That hot, sick feeling in her stomach came back again. Daddy called it shame; Mommy called it guilt. Maybe this could be both.

Falling made them sound scared, too, but a different kind of scared. A scared-for-me way, not a scared-for-someone-else. The floor put itself back together, wood reconnecting, skin sealing over an open wound. She might not have thought much of this a few days earlier, or even an hour ago, but hearing her parents talk that way made Helena look nervously toward the front door.

Don't worry. They're perfectly fine. They just got a little confused, so I put them in the basement for a while. Like a timeout. Even parents need one sometimes. You don't want them to take you away from me, do you?

She shook her head, because when grown-ups ask you something, there's a correct answer, and even if she didn't really know if The House was an adult, she knew it expected a certain response. Helena told The House she wanted to stay. Her brain didn't agree, but she didn't like the basement. It smelled funny, and that's where spiders live. She'd wait up here for Mommy and Daddy and The House to get along again. They'd be a happy family soon enough.

Chapter 18

Charlotte and Elijah lost track of time. The basement didn't have windows, so they couldn't see outside. Their phones both died within an hour of getting trapped in the basement, and neither had service. Searching for a signal probably killed off the batteries. Whatever. They didn't have a plan anyway. How could they get around this?

The House could seal the doors and windows, block their cell signal, and apparently break the floors and walls to pieces, then put them back together again.

The House heard their every whisper, and maybe it could read, too. They had no way of knowing. Charlotte could write down a mundane phrase and ask if it knew what the paper said, but it would lie. It obviously would. The House would know they wanted to plan something, and it would tell them it couldn't read so it could circumvent their plans.

As an attempt at a semblance of privacy, she set the washer and dryer to re-run their current loads. She hadn't finished the laundry, after all, and could de-wrinkle without drawing suspicion. Elijah guessed they'd been down there about eighteen hours, based on his hunger, and having fallen asleep. Their daughter hummed and bounced around upstairs, making clanging noises in the kitchen. If anything went wrong, they wouldn't be able to help her. Maybe she already had help.

"I hope she's feeding herself healthy food." Charlotte kept her eyes trained on the ceiling.

"She's five." Elijah sat on the floor with his chin resting on his fists. "Then again, we don't exactly have junk food lying around."

"Still, she could be, I don't know, stuffing her face full of cheese and bread. What if she isn't getting nutrients?" Her pacing scuffed her feet against the floor, stirring up little pockets of dust.

"I'll be sure to stop by the store and get some multivitamins soon." Groaning, he stretched backward, a series of pops echoing from his spine as he stretched. "Guess it's not all bad that I took a week off, though, huh?"

"You mean, so your staff doesn't wonder where you are, since you can't call in about playing hooky? Think it's kinda the opposite here, babe. If you were supposed to come in, they might send someone to investigate."

He knew she was right. Tilting back, he stretched out on the floor, listening to his stomach growl. He had some of the most diligent, respectful, reliable staff members in the business, which meant they wouldn't dare bother him on a vacation day, no matter the reason. A sick day, maybe, if only to wish him wellness and verify he wouldn't be in, but not a planned day off.

Charlotte needed a vacation from all this. They all did, but most clearly her. As a mark of how absorbed he'd been in his work, Elijah hadn't noticed how pale she'd become. Shadows gathered under her eyes like they were ready to wage war, putting an end to the last little bit of strength she had left in her withered frame. She'd lost some weight from the stress of losing James, but now, he could almost see her ribcage through her shirt. Her hair, once more brilliant than straw in the dawn sunlight, all bronze and gold and fire, now hung in limp, brownish strands. That meant he probably looked worse. Everyone knew his wife put his looks to shame—not that he was ugly, just an average person standing next to Venus—but the busy nature of his life lately, and his general disdain for bothering with mirrors, hair styles, or nice clothes, meant his normally disheveled appearance had probably degraded to 'trash.'

They both stewed in the private silences of their wandering minds until a knock resounded at the door. Each jerked a head up, but in different directions. Elijah looked toward the basement door, while Charlotte looked to the front of the house, where the sound had actually come from. Little footsteps pattered over. Hinges squeaked as the door opened, and Paulina, Charlotte's reiki friend, came clomping inside, loud as ever.

"Oh, hi there, Helena! Look how big you're getting! Is your mother home? I wanted to talk to her about this great new tincture I got that wards off stress. Stress is such a pesky thing, you know. It clings to you, like mosquitos, or a heavy fog, and just bleh, drains your energy, makes you so sluggish! Figure it will help her shoulder to get that monkey off her back. There's a reason we have sayings like that, and it's because they're true. People manifest their stress on their shoulders and it becomes an actual psychic weight that—"

"Mommy's upstairs!" Helena yelled. Charlotte looked over at Elijah, eyes practically bulging out of her skull, but he laughed. Despite the situation, he couldn't help appreciate that Helena found her as painfully annoying as he did.

"Aren't you worried?" Charlotte hissed.

"Worried? About what?"

"Why she told her I'm upstairs. Why would she do that?"

Now Elijah worried too. They didn't have to sit in contemplative anxiety for long. A sudden snap of floorboards echoed through the house, and a shrill yelp preceded a heavy thudding down the main staircase. He counted one, two, four thuds, then a moment of silence where he thought she'd stopped. The silence broke with a sickening crack. No, she hadn't stopped falling, she must've bounced into the air, and that sound was her skull breaking against the stone landing.

The basement door swung open.

Charlotte charged up before he'd managed to uncoil his now-stiff legs. Sitting on the ground was a young man's game, not the type of position a business owner and father wanted to be in. By the time he stumbled up the rickety stairs and into the living room, his wife had clutched Helena to her. Helena allowed her mom to hug her but showed no interest in returning the gesture. She did look a little nervous. Just a little. Her gaze flicked over to meet his, then over toward the stairs.

Crumpled at the foot, Paulina lay in a tangled heap of gemstones and broken bones. Her leg twisted at a terrible angle. Her head practically sat backward on her shoulders, bleeding from a fracture he couldn't see.

This presents you with an interesting choice, doesn't it?

Elijah looked up at the walls. Charlotte saw that he heard it but gave no indication she heard it too.

Your wife is busy consoling a child who isn't interested in her parenting anymore. You, on the other hand, have a duty to this family. The man of the house, right? An occupant once lived here who said a man had particular duties, and particular needs. In exchange for, say, mowing the lawn, he'd demand food and sex. Refusal resulted in a slap, if his wife was lucky. Don't worry, though. I'm not the monster you think I am. I killed him, too, and my oh my, was she grateful. So grateful, in fact, that she did some remodeling to my specifications—including the stone at the bottom of the stairs. Made it far easier to dispose of nuisances.

He knew he'd turned white, maybe verging on green, but didn't care. What could he say? What could he, or anyone, or anything, do? He'd consider a priest, but that felt ridiculous—not to mention that he couldn't leave, or even dial out of the house.

Your choice, Elijah—can I call you Eli?—is whether to bury her quietly in the backyard, or call the police. Notify authorities, and you'll be suspects in a wrongful death, which will make it extremely difficult to leave. Bury her out back, and you'll be able to move without the police caring—until the realtor or new occupant gets suspicious about the freshly dug mound of dirt in the otherwise pristine, green backyard. Unless you're going to go out, get a drum full of acid, and dissolve her body, or seal her in the concrete at one of your sites like a mafioso, I don't see you having many other options.

Hands balled into fists, he briefly wondered if he'd hurt it by punching the walls. Well, hurt it more than he'd hurt himself. In the brief window of time before it struck back, probably killing him.

"This is my house, damn it. Our house. Me, my wife, my god damn child. We live here."

No, you live in MY house. I was here first, and I'll outlast all of you—whether you move away or are removed by the appropriate responders. Whatever happens, it'll be your choice, and you'll bear the consequences.

He almost replied, but The House cut him off.

Although, before you go calling the police, you may want to consider the fact that Thanksgiving is in four days, and Helena already emailed everyone on your wife's behalf about what they should bring, and how grateful you are for them to be coming. Canceling now would be... suspicious. The kind of suspicious that might make one of Charlotte's more well-to-do relatives investigate if, on top of that, you were to suddenly move again.

"What's going on?" Charlotte asked. "What's The House saying?"

He turned to Helena instead. "Sweetie, did The House ask you to email people?"

"Uh-huh," she nodded. "The House said you were going to be mean and try to take me away, and I don't want to go, so if I did like it asked, I'd get to stay here." She crossed her little arms in front of her chest and turned away from him.

Yet another reason as to why you can't leave.

"Apparently, we're in for an interesting Thanksgiving," Elijah said. He and Charlotte exchanged a look, sharing one of their brief moments of complete, unspoken understanding. They did have a plan. A bad one, but a plan nonetheless.

I recommend digging in the night, when there won't be prying eyes. If you really want to hide the body, put her six feet under, then a stray dog or cat about two feet deep. Cover both bodies with lime to keep the smell down. Anyone who goes investigating will think you lost a pet, rather than concealed a crime.

"Why do you know that?" He looked up at the ceiling, unable to shake the feeling of this dark presence looming over them.

Helena responded instead. "Don't you get it, Daddy? The House knows everything. That's why we should never, ever leave."

The parents looked at her. Charlotte loosened her grip. Elijah wondered if they even had a shovel, or if he'd have to go get one.

This must be why the house went through so many renovations and remodels.

"Fine. Fuck it, whatever." Helena recoiled at her father's profanity, knowing that this was a bad word, but having never heard him say it on purpose before. This, above all, was the first time she stopped to think something might be really, really wrong. "I'll bury her outback. Guess I need to run to the store. Shovel, lime, and seeds." Winter was coming. The grass wouldn't grow. That didn't really matter though.

Good. And don't forget grout cleaner. I don't want my landing getting stained.

Chapter 19

Marcy the Realtor called back that evening, finally, and gave Elijah the full list of death disclosures. She started two minutes into the call, not stopping until minute twenty-eight. The call only lasted twenty-nine. He thanked her, did not inform her of the newest death on the property, and bid her a happy Thanksgiving.

A few years back, he'd met a woman equal parts trouble and troubled, whose eyes were sparks for her gasoline personality. Any wrong move could set her off, but she was good to the people she liked, few that they were. Elijah had been once such person, which is how he knew her signature drink was The Wake-Up Call, a shot of the smokiest scotch she could get her hands on poured into a strong black coffee. At the time, it seemed like a very dumb and unhealthy idea. Now, at three AM, hands blistered and dirty from the one labor he never thought he'd have to do, he appreciated having run into her. All this time later, she still managed to be a good friend, via a toxic brew that burned like the hell he'd surely go to when he died. Nothing made him feel better about the decomposing woman in his backyard, but the drink dulled his nerves, quieting the howl of pain that had replaced the beating of his heart.

Charlotte said she'd take care of the rest. He couldn't do anymore. First he missed his son's death, then watched Seamus die, then learned that there are supernatural creatures in this world and that one had taken over parenting his daughter, and now he hastily buried a corpse in the backyard. With lime, as The House recommended. Without the pet to throw off those who might go digging.

Four AM rolled around, then five, and he didn't get his wife, or even get up to piss. He only moved far enough to get more coffee. He didn't need to sleep to know his dreams would replay the thudding of Paulina's body, or the snap of her neck. Elijah couldn't risk seeing the cold, dead stare again, or feeling the way her stiffening body resisted his attempts to move her, as if still fighting for survival, protesting the shameful way he hid her from the world, like a child kicking a loose sneaker under his bed.

Funny, how some loss is so great that it radiates, isn't it? One person experiences a tragedy, and all those around are affected, too. Paulina lost her life. What did you lose?

He didn't reply. He took another long sip, his scotch half drained. Becoming a parent usually reduces alcohol tolerance—you just don't have time to knock back beers anymore, so your liver forgets what it's like—but this, right now, this purgatory where he'd wait until the devil his parents warned about finally dragged him into the flames, this was the sobering shit that's just a little too damn real. This is what drives people crazy, and the booze, it puts a haze over reality, makes it like you're watching a movie, so you can keep your eyes open through an ending you know you don't want to watch.

The clock struck six, and his wife came down the stairs, walking quietly over to his side. "You're still up? I thought maybe you fell asleep on the couch. I… I couldn't sleep either. Would've come down if I knew you were sitting here."

Her gaze fell on the coffee cup, then the alcohol. He'd mentioned Wake-Up Calls to her before, but neither of them ever drank one. Just a passing anecdote about a weird person he met one time, while doing another odd job in another odd place.

"Eli? Are you okay?" She put a hand on his shoulder.

Without a word, he turned to her, buried his face in her stomach, and cried.

Chapter 20

Helena laughed downstairs in the living room, while Charlotte and Elijah sat on their bed. It had been made explicitly clear to them that they weren't her primary guardians anymore. Oh, they could still make food and take her to school, but The House would lock the other parent inside, and they couldn't go through the little rituals that really determine what a family means. No more TV together, no board games, no bedtime stories. If they built a pillow fort, it was only because The House couldn't, and Helena wasn't physically able to. Whenever they crossed paths, their daughter gave them a curious stare, the way a researcher might peer at a new species of butterfly he'd pinned to a dartboard, watching it wriggle and writhe and try in vain to fly.

"I should've known. Should've been… aware, I guess. That this place was wrong." Elijah's cold, distant tone sounded as empty as he felt. Charlotte hadn't seen him eat in over a day. Two, technically. Forty-eight hours passed between them being cast down into the basement, and this moment, where they sat on the bed together. All that scotch hit him hard, but he didn't sleep. Wept, silently, and sometimes not so silently, but didn't sleep.

"Eli, you couldn't possibly have known. I should've told you."

He shook his head and left the room, a hand at his waist, holding up pants that had fit him perfectly only a few days earlier. She heard him shuffling around in Helena's room, and when a few minutes passed without another sound, she followed him in. Her husband sat on their daughter's bed, looking at a stack of papers. Children's drawings, with Helena's messy, child-like, but still recognizable scrawl. A parent always recognizes their kid's writing, even if every kid writes equally terribly.

"Remember that first time you took her to the store, just a few weeks after we moved in?" His hands shook, rustling the pages. This might've been from fear and apprehension, or it might've just been from hunger and low blood sugar. "I found one of these. She'd drawn this and left it at the empty place setting. At her tea table."

Charlotte looked over at the little table, where all the chairs had occupants, except for one. She'd only connected the empty spot to The House on Halloween, and even then, Helena practically had to slap her in the face and yell, "I hear it too!" for her to get the message. Their little girl had made it so obvious. Charlotte had been so distracted lately, she completely missed every sign, and every little suggestion. The House was right. She'd been selfish. Distracted. Too lost in her own problems, too distracted by the death of one child to care about the one that lived.

"These drawings are all of people who used to live here. People who died here. All of them, except the one I saw, back then. This is the one I saw." He turned a picture around. Helena had drawn their house, from a front-facing view, as if standing on the sidewalk outside. Three stick figures held hands, their arms in such a way that it looked like The House was smiling. Instead of second story windows, she'd drawn eyes. Big, bloodshot eyes that wouldn't have belonged on a human being, let alone a two-story building. Yet there it loomed, clear as day, the deranged domicile made manifest by a child's drawing. This giant, glow-in-the-dark clue might've tipped her off sooner, but she couldn't be sure. Everything looks clear in hindsight. It's possible that, if she'd seen it, she would've shrugged it off as another act of childhood personification. If Mr. Bear could drink tea, why couldn't a house have eyes?

That's what she would've told herself, anyway. It'd only been two months, but her body hurt in a way that screamed it had been years. Every bone cried with weariness, her heart struggling to beat as her chest tightened. Eli was suffering enough, though. She couldn't let this show; she couldn't place her burdens on his already aching shoulders.

"I wish we'd seen the rest." He shook his head. His eyes, bloodshot and circled by blue-black rings, weren't much different from The House's eyes in Helena's drawing. "Here."

He extended a hand, and she took the pages. Each had a different picture with a story either underneath or on the back. They were simple little tales, with the lack of detail most children's stories had, letting the image do the work.

The first showed a man hanging by a rope in the master bedroom's closet, slumped on the ground but clearly asphyxiated. She'd written, "Mr. Bennon liked money, but he liked gambling more. He played every game; he played fast and loose. He couldn't stop losing, so he wound up poor. The only way out of his debt was a noose."

Page two showed a woman dead in the basement, reaching up toward the closed door, the stairs, and her legs, broken. "Jenny Polinsky was known for her anger. She'd beat up her husband, then yell at her kids. To everyone else, she was a danger. The House locked her away, and her body it hid."

Another: two people dead on the living room floor, faces green. "Larry and Susan were not very kind. They sold bad insurance, and good people died. One night, while drunk out of their minds, they wound up drinking cyanide."

Charlotte shut her eyes, turning her head away. "God, are these the stories it's been telling her? Why? Why would it do this to our little girl?"

She asked for stories with a little more impact.

Her stomach roiled at the sudden intrusion on what she'd thought to be a semi-private moment. "I don't believe you. My sweet little girl didn't ask for these horror stories." Elijah looked up in alarm as she addressed The House, but kept quiet, clearly not wanting to be involved any more than he already was.

She did. Every single night. She said James's death made it hard to believe in fairy tales, but you just kept telling the same old stories of princesses and fairies and happy endings she knew she'd never have, so I told her a few stories of my own.

"You killed these people, didn't you? But you portray yourself as the savior."

Naturally. History is told by the last person standing as the fallen grow cold on the ground. Who else, then, would tell these stories? Who's to say I'm not, in fact, the savior?

"Probably the people who died here. I doubt they'd appreciate your so-called salvation."

Yet, I freed so many others, and protected more still. The people who've lived here were not good people. They got by on insurance fraud and embezzlement, abused their spouses and children, used drugs like lovers and used lovers like drugs. You call me a monster for having killed, but I'm no murderer. I'm a sentinel. All guards must kill, when there is a threat to their people.

"Growing stronger all the while, right? Each death adds to your influence?"

Yes. Those who witness death can hear me; those who die here become part of me.

She'd never thrown up from stress or fear or anger, but this made her come close. Swallowing that feeling back, she said, "Then why? Why would you… What do you want with our daughter?"

All stories of those trapped by unseen forces involve sacrifice. A life willingly given can set even the most bound souls free. I knew you'd pose a hassle. A child, though? Children are easy to manipulate. She'll give herself over to me soon enough.

If any one moment in her life would've stopped Charlotte's heart, this would've been it. Not her mother's death, not her father leaving, not being adopted, nor any of the many times as a child she'd been told she was either overly imaginative or outright insane. All her anxieties and sneaking suspicions about The House had been confirmed: it didn't simply want her daughter here, it wanted to kill her.

Her flight or fight instincts went wild, each demanding action, yelling at her to run away, to fight back, but she knew she couldn't do either. Instinct slammed into the wall of unassailable logic. They couldn't leave, because The House could seal the doors. They couldn't kill it, because it was a fucking house.

Or, maybe they could. A storm cloud gathering in her mind threw lightning, sending a surge to her every cell. There's more than one way to leave a house.

Willing her hands to stop shaking, Charlotte let out a couple breaths, trying to find her center. She'd need to stay focused, and she'd need to keep Eli out of this, for his mental sake if nothing else. This meant asking a few final questions of their residence, but first, she flipped through Helena's drawings. She found the one she sought soon enough.

A woman lay on her back in the open door to her dishwasher, blood pooling on the floor. A man stood over her, while a child sat under the table, staring. Beneath the scene, Helena wrote, "Darleen had too much love for just one man, so she'd spend time in bed with whoever came by. When caught, she swore she wouldn't do it again, and proved it, since she was the first to die."

Nothing about this fazed her. She'd been through too much, felt such an overwhelming surge of emotions through the past few days, that reading this about her mother had no impact. It could've been a grocery list. Charlotte moved back here to chase the past, but now, after all this, The House had inadvertently given her the best gift she could've asked for: closure. What did the past matter, when her family's future was in jeopardy?

"Is this true?" she asked.

Your mother cheated on your father, yes. Only with one man, and only a few times, so maybe I exaggerated when telling Helena, but I suppose I took some creative liberties in making sure the story was worthwhile. Don't worry. I didn't tell her that Darleen was your mother. To her, this was just another bedtime tale. And no, her death had nothing to do with me.

She nodded. That answer sucked, but it was good enough.

"Let's put these back," Charlotte said, motioning to the pictures. "I have to go shopping."

Elijah's jaw hung open like a door clinging to one rusty hinge. "Shopping?"

"Yes, dear. Thanksgiving is in two days, and we have twenty people coming. We have to make sure we're ready."

Chapter 21

Thanksgiving Day, and Charlotte felt truly thankful.

In a bad situation, it can be easy to lose hope, but a fresh perception turns everything around. Getting lost in a new perspective is what helps people find themselves.

When you're trapped, you either accept your cage, or find a way out. Aron Ralston cut off his own arm to escape the circumstances that would've otherwise killed him, and he became famous for it. The House was right about that much: sacrifice sets you free.

Charlotte opened the door, hoping her parents wouldn't see past the inch-thick make-up cake she'd smashed her face into early that day. Keeping up appearances meant dealing with her literal appearance. There was no hope for Elijah, whose tired, rumbly, old-mountain voice and weathered face wouldn't have looked right with any shade of foundation. People would have to deal with his droopy eyes and occasional snoring.

His disposition, and mental health overall, hadn't improved over the past few days. She'd convinced him to limit his Wake-Up Calls to one per hour and hoped her parents—who arrived in formal evening wear that would've looked excessive at a five-star hotel—didn't notice.

"Charlotte, my dear, hello." Her mother, Michelle, leaned in, giving her a kiss on both cheeks. Stiff blonde curls poked into the sides of her head, suggesting she'd spent a bit too long at the salon getting ready. Jacob, her father, held up a glass bowl with plastic wrap over the top, displaying the salad they'd made. Or, more likely, bought, then dumped into a fancy container.

"How are you?" Jacob never asked how people were unless they'd been through hard times. Though he didn't exactly lack empathy, he certainly didn't care about day-to-day minutia, so he made a point not to give people the invitation to talk unless they really seemed like they'd need to.

"We're okay." Charlotte nodded to him, welcoming them inside. "We're okay," she repeated, for her own benefit more than his.

"Good to hear." He patted her on the shoulder. He rarely hugged Michelle. His children, not at all. Adopted or otherwise. "Anything we can do to help?"

She shook her head and introduced them to Elijah's siblings, who'd come dressed in normal clothing, all jeans and t-shirts and plain skirts, which made that a strange looking crowd. The children had gathered under a large pillow fort in the corner of the room, where they huddled in secret, telling stories and genuinely believing the adults weren't allowed to join them. This small modicum of false authority had been Charlotte's idea.

"I believe everyone's here now," she said to her husband, who was in the kitchen, failing horribly at his attempt to make mashed potatoes. There were more half-churned spuds on the counter than in his mixing bowl. "My parents, your parents, your four siblings, their three kids, my sister and her wife, my aunt and uncle… Yeah, that should be everyone."

"Pffft, everyone. Not everyone, is it?" He hiccupped, looking forlorn at the bowl.

"Look, we… we have enough to deal with right now, don't you think?" She felt guilty for chastising him. He had every right to think about James and want him to be here. Self-pity wouldn't help them though.

"I guess." Abandoning the potatoes, he weaved his way back to the living room, where she heard him plop down on the couch next to her sister-in-law. She couldn't hear what he asked and didn't want to know. Distractions wouldn't exactly hurt.

Wouldn't be very hard for me to drop your whole family down below, you know. You read Helena's little legend about the woman who died down there. Do you know how sticky she was when they found her? More puddle than person, really. They cleaned her out of here with a vacuum.

That might've been a bad time to start thinking about what kind of cheese to melt for the kids to pour over their broccoli. She turned away, knowing her face began approaching the stems' shade of green, and stared deeply into the potatoes instead. Smooth, unsurprising, unassuming potatoes, a stabilizing factor for every

American holiday. She couldn't think of one USA-exclusive celebration that wasn't marked by the dish.

I'm glad you came to your senses, though. Really. Helena needs a good home. A nice, stable environment. The more trouble you cause, the more unreliable this environment might get.

The floor buckled underneath her, so she grabbed onto the counter.

"Char? You okay?" Her sister, Abigail, had entered, giving her a confused look. Her dark eyebrow curled its way toward her artificially light hair, contouring her acne-scarred forehead with an array of wrinkles.

"Y-yeah, Abby, I'm fine. Go relax. I'll give you a shout if I need anything."

She snorted. "Good call. Don't think your husband's up for much tonight." With a sidelong glance back into the living room, she added, "I know you guys have been through a lot lately, but it seems like everything's rougher than usual. You sure you're okay?"

Charlotte nodded. "Right as rain, sis."

Abigail gave a big show of sniffing the kitchen air. "Well it sure smells like you've got everything under control. But..." She sniffed again. Before she could speak, Charlotte walked over and ushered her out, almost pushing, saying things were fine, but she needed space.

Physical distance is not so different from emotional distance. Is that the real reason why you moved back here? A piece of your heart went missing long ago, and you thought you'd find it within these walls.

"Don't be ridiculous. I moved here to find out about Mom and get to know you a bit."

Now you know. Is it everything you dreamed of, Charlotte? Am I the angel you sought? Is the truth of your mother—that she was a cuckolding klutz who ruined a wonderful marriage—the ending you wanted?

"Shut up."

Of course not. No one wants to hear such terrible things about their family, especially when that family isn't around to defend itself anymore. But, sadly, you follow in your parents' footsteps. Your mother thought the world revolved around her, as did you, by moving here under the premise that only you could hear me, and I was a private little part of your life—a secret you could lock away, and turn to only when you needed it. Your father was a coward who ran at the first sign of trouble, as you tried to, in threatening to take my Helena away from me because you didn't like that fact that she talks to me, too.

Charlotte told herself The House didn't know what it talked about, and told herself this as many times as she could, because it didn't, and what could it know, anyway? Spirit in the walls or sentient structure, The House only knew what it observed.

You should answer the door.

She straightened up, looking back toward the living room. No one knocked, and the bell hadn't rung. After putting the potatoes back down, her own attempts at mashing woefully inadequate, she returned to the living room. That's when the bell rang.

If The House laid another trick or trap, this didn't seem to make much sense. Luring her into, what, opening the door? What would that serve, other than distracting her from the plans in the kitchen? She didn't intend to really serve the food she'd been preparing—it wouldn't be cooked. Not properly, anyway.

"We espectin' someone else?" Elijah slurred.

Charlotte shook her head. Edging her way around his siblings, who didn't seem to have noticed the sound, she took a look through the peephole. A man stood outside. She didn't recognize him but opened up anyway.

"Hello. Can I help you?" She looked the man over. He stood a few inches taller than her, with an extra weight around the middle, gray stubble, and hair that had been neatly combed, but still clearly spent a lot of time in an unkempt swirl. She put him at maybe late fifties, though his weary eyes and deep wrinkles made him seem many years older.

He tried to speak but couldn't.

"Are you okay, sir? Do you need me to call someone?"

But the longer he stared, the harder her heart pounded. She wasn't afraid of him. More like The House—however it had brought this man here, or for what purpose. Nothing good could come of this surprise. Instinct already provided a hazard of a guess. She didn't like its answer.

"Charlotte?" The man said.

Her gut knotted. Intuition, spot on as ever, hadn't let her down. Out of all the people to arrive on her doorstep, this had to be literally the worst possible person.

"Dad?"

A second chin quivered as he held back twenty-five years' worth of overdue tears. Naturally, The House invited him, not that she knew how.

"I know I don't des—"

Charlotte cut him off. "Please. Come on in."

Despite how odd it felt, and knowing her adoptive parents were watching, she opened her arms. He moved in to hug her, clearly not sure if it was the right gesture either, but too many emotions raged in her heart for Charlotte to do anything but move on autopilot. She wrapped him up tight and decided, intellectually, that gratitude was the best choice. On Thanksgiving, you show appreciation for what you have, no matter how much time you have left with it, or how much time you've lost along the way.

"Dear? Who's this?" Michelle said, moving to her side, with Jacob on her heel.

They released each other. "Mom, Dad, this is… well, my dad. Uh…" She turned to him, "I'm sorry. I don't know your name."

"George," he said, snapping his light gray eyes off the ground to look into theirs.

"Hm. You think you can walk back into her life after all the pain you caused her?" Jacob said, eyeing her father up the way a tiger eyes a gazelle.

"Only if she'll let me." Jacob seemed to like this answer, so George added, "I owe her too much to ever repay. If she wants me here, I stay. If she doesn't, I'll… go." Pain wracked his face when he said this, but he did a passable job at hiding it.

As horrible as the scene felt, in some ways, it moved her to tears. Good tears. It must've been hard for him to decide to come here, let alone on a day when he had to anticipate more than a little animosity aimed his way. Maybe he'd finally become the father she'd needed him to be twenty-five years earlier: someone who'd stand his ground and fight.

Then another expression crossed his face. Confusion, mixed with a hint of dread, and some twinges of remorse thrown in for good measure. She knew what this meant. After all, he saw her mother die, too. God only knew what The House started saying.

"I, uh, have to go check on the food. Would you like to help?" She emphasized help, hoping he'd realize she wasn't talking about food. He did, nodded, and followed. On the way, Elijah looked up from the couch, then heaved himself out of the depression he'd sunk into, chasing after them.

"Hey, hey, hey," Elijah said, having caught up with them. He couldn't stand too straight but did his best to seem intimidating toward the stranger in his home. "Who's this guy?"

"This… is my dad." She couldn't get used to the phrase. "Guess he, uh, is back now, and I'm happy he's here."

Neither of them had drank heavily since their youth, so she had no idea what to expect for his reaction. Fortunately, rather than anything crazy, he knelt down at George's feet. "Welcome to my home, sir. It's been a pleasure to know your--*hic*--your daughter. She's the fuckin' best." He took George's hand and kissed it, much to George's fleeting amusement.

"Please forgive him. It's been a long week, and he's pretty drunk." Then, to Eli, she said, "Honey, why don't you—honey. Honey!" His eyes drooped shut. He almost toppled over, asleep, but she took his face in her hands. "Wake up, sleepyhead. I need you to go back in the living room and talk to our guests, okay?" She kissed his forehead and helped him up. "Just coffee for you from now on. No more alcohol until dinner."

"Yes, my love. I'm the best at talking, savvy?"

Elijah swaggered out with what he undoubtedly thought was a good Johnny Depp impression, though he came off more like a Monty Python character.

George looked over. "He seems like a good man. Goofy, but good."

"He's the best I could've asked for." Tears spilled from her eyes. Her father looked understandably worried, but she didn't give him a chance to speak. "You hear it, don't you? The House?"

"The—The House? What do you mean?" He glanced toward the living room.

"Whatever it's calling itself, don't believe it. It's not mom, or you, or a demon, or, or anything, really. It's just… The House. There's something in the walls, here. It's been trying to lure my daughter away to—to kill her. I think. But you're not crazy. I saw that look on your face like maybe you thought you were, but you're not. There's an old presence here, and it hates everyone."

His mouth stayed set in a resolute line. He nodded, as if he'd heard all this before, or maybe heard so much insanity elsewhere that this barely bothered him. "I have a granddaughter?"

She almost laughed, but it came out as a repressed sob. "Yeah. Yeah, you do. Her name is Helena, and she's the sweetest little girl you'll ever meet. You, uh… You had a grandson, too."

"Had," he repeated, gray eyes cast back toward the floor, head eternally bowed in penance for a sin he knew he'd never fully be absolved of. "I see. I wish I'd been here." They stood in silence, then concern crossed his brow. "Do I smell—"

She held a finger to his lips and wrapped him up in another tight hug. "After all this time, I really thought I'd have been mad at you. Or yelled at you. Or something. All I know is that I'm glad you're here. Really, really glad. So… let's just… be okay. Let's let tonight, let's let right now, be enough, okay?"

He held her back without a word, but she could feel him trying not to cry.

When she pulled away, she cleared her throat a few times. Once wasn't enough. "Here. I have a few things left to do, and I don't actually need help. Why don't I introduce you two, and you can keep an eye on her, make sure she stays out there, out of the way, while Eli... I don't know, stays drunk on the couch. Sound good?"

George gave her a somber nod, knowing it had become his duty to say yes, no matter the request. Charlotte smiles through watery eyes, then blotted them dry on a dish towel, leading him out into the living room. She 'knocked' on the pillow fort's flap, asking Helena to come out for a second. She did, her tiny frame squirming on out of the covers, eyes widening with surprise at the stranger before her.

"Helena, this is my dad. The dad I had a long time ago. He's your grandpa. Well, another grandpa."

She knew the stink eye she got from Michelle, but as George knelt down to say hello, she got pure approval from Jacob and Abigail. Abby's wife was attempting to entertain Eli's half-cocked conversation about why the annual dog show should replace the summer Olympics. The rest of their relatives milled about in a happy holiday buzz, a glass of wine in almost every hand.

Charlotte walked back into the kitchen, paced a little, and got out a lighter. She'd learned a thing or two about The House. The House learned a lot about her. No matter how omnipotent, though, it wouldn't ever learn all her secrets. It had made the mistake of telling her all of its.

What are you doing?

The House knew something was wrong. She knew it knew and didn't care.

Charlotte, answer me.

She took a deep breath, feeling her head spin, and said, "You can taunt me, torture me, lock me up in my own house, spy on me from every corner, and hear every word I say. You were never going to let us go. That was never an option. Wasn't for all the other occupants, wasn't for us. Right?"

You're being strange. What are you planning?

"That's why Helena could never really be your child—why she'd never give herself over to you. A real parent knows you can't hold a kid too closely. Even when they're young, you have to know when to let go."

She flicked the lighter on just as her ears pricked up to tiny footsteps and sputtering gasps. Her head turned as Helena ran toward her, panic in her eyes. George chased after her, arms outstretched, snatching her up right as the lighter's flame caught the gas fumes that had been filling the kitchen since she cut the line earlier that evening.

The House had been busy playing with Helena. It didn't see her do it. She didn't talk about doing it. And The House had no sense of smell.

Fire filled the kitchen. Everything went red. Then it all went black.

Chapter 22

What did you do?

Charlotte groaned, coughing dust from her lungs and throat, her vision creeping back in by degrees. The lights were out, but fire kept the room bright.

Someone screamed in the background. Heat burned her hands, but her torso felt cold. Elijah knelt in the living room, just beyond the threshold to the kitchen, staring at her, face blank. Shock and alcohol probably dulled him enough that, maybe, he'd think he was dreaming. He'd spend the rest of his life trying to wake up.

A few feet away, a wriggling drew her attention. Helena pried herself out of George's grasp. Shards of metal from the exploded stove had pierced through his neck. His face appeared peaceful, like he'd known what would happen if he came back here. Maybe she knew it, too.

Charlotte? Sweetie?

The House. It didn't sound the same as before. Not the cold, whispery, vengeful voice of a ghoul coming to kill you in the dead of night, but just… there. Almost like a regular person, but still without a discernable age or gender.

As her vision came back, Helena ran to her father's arms, looking back at Charlotte. Charlotte looked down at the three-inch-wide piece of metal impaling her torso, just under her left breast. It might've missed her lung and diaphragm, but the cold in her chest was spreading, and the kitchen walls were on fire, and Michelle screamed that the front door wouldn't open.

Why did you do this? I know you wanted to hurt me, but you hurt everyone. Yourself, your father, daughter, husband… What kind of person do you have to be to do this? Who the hell are you?

A massive hole in the supporting wall marked where the stove had been. The ceiling turned black and started to buckle under the heat. Abigail ran toward them all, but Elijah, so thoroughly sobered that he might never be drunk again, held an arm out to keep her back.

"Open the door. Please." Her hands started shaking.

I can't. I've come too far.

The House fell silent, at least for her. Helena shook her head, beginning to cry. She turned around to hug her dad tight around the neck, then looked back toward the stove. "You're not safe. You locked Mommy and Daddy in the basement, and now you hurt Mommy, and Grandpa, too. You lied."

The rest kept up their chatter and commotion, but their little family shared a moment of silence. Rightful order had been restored. She got her daughter back.

But good parents know when to let go.

"Take me," Charlotte said.

"Mommy?"

You?

"You said… a life willingly given. You didn't say… whose." Blood filled her mouth. Ash and pennies scented every breath, her vision turning a red that had nothing to do with the flames. The ceiling buckled further, a loud groan echoing from upstairs as furniture shifted.

"Charlotte, no!" Elijah said. Abby backed away, knowing whatever was going on here lay far beyond her ability to intervene.

Why give your life? Why you, if you went through all this trouble?

She laughed, spitting out some crimson in the process. "I thought it'd blow a hole to outside. Didn't think… the walls were so strong."

Well, they are. I would know, wouldn't I?

"Yeah. Guess you would. But I'm dying anyway, and this started with me. Should end that way."

…If you're certain… then I guess I was right. Your life came full circle.

"Yeah. You saved my life. Now you'll take it."

Helena broke free of her dad's embrace, running to Charlotte. She knelt down and put her hands on her mom's face. "No! You can't, you have to come with us. You have to! We're a family!"

Seeing the pain in her daughter's eyes was worse than the metal running her through. It hurt in a deep way that would scar, if she were going to live past the next few minutes, but she wasn't going to. She'd always wanted to die peacefully in her sleep, but life's not about what you want. Her life most of all.

"Sweetie, listen. I want to. But I can't." She reached up and tucked a loose strand of Helena's hair back behind her ear. "You're so young. This'll hurt, maybe for the rest of your life. But please, do the one thing I couldn't: Learn to live without your mommy."

The girl shook her head hard, leaning down, grabbing onto Charlotte's neck and holding tight even as the ceiling behind her cracked from the heat. If she noticed, she didn't seem to care. Elijah edged over, pulling his daughter away.

"Eli. I loved you so much. I'm sorry things happened this way. You deserved so much better." She reached up and held the hand that wasn't restraining their child. To Helena, she added, "It'll be fine one day, baby. I promise. I'll tell James you said hi. Just don't come looking for us. You've seen… how that will end."

Elijah stood up, holding his daughter tight to his chest as she thrashed around, calling out for her mom. She looked over his shoulder as they ran back toward the door, and when Charlotte nodded to the burning ceiling, that front door swung wide open. Their families rushed out. He lingered, long enough to look back, then stepped onto the front porch, shutting the door behind him.

"Okay. Now what?"

A thunk drew her attention to the pantry. The crawlspace door had opened. Beyond, there was only darkness. The lights from the fire didn't cross that gap. No light would. She didn't know everything, but she knew that. Knew it in the tremble of her faltering heartbeat.

Charlotte dragged herself, one arm length at a time, toward the opening.

I could've been better to you.

"Yeah." She paused to spit blood on the floor. Her vision began fading, but adrenaline gave her a boost. "Everyone could be… better to each other. Human or otherwise."

I was… wrong… about your father.

"Doesn't matter now." She reached the little entryway and stuck her hand in. Darkness enveloped her at the threshold, cutting off her visibility. She withdrew, saw her fingers again, and stuck them in, losing sight, as if plunging them into murky water.

Charlotte? …Thank you.

She could say "Screw you" and stay put, bleed to death on the floor now that everyone had escaped, but no. She didn't want her last act to be one of spite. The House needed her help, the way she'd once needed its help. Time to repay the favor.

With the last dredges of her strength, Charlotte crawled into the darkness, and the door slid shut behind her.

About the Author

Kevin Holton is a cyborg, editor, novelist, and award-winning screenwriter. When not reading and writing, he can be found gaming or meditating.

Other HellBound Books Titles
Available at: www.hellboundbookspublishing.com

Dig Two Graves

In the blurred lines between good and evil - who will win?

Jezebel White is a court-appointed psychologist who runs an underground human trafficking empire.

In order to justify her nefarious actions to her conscience, she selects victims based solely upon whom she deems immoral.

Now, she finds herself being framed for a crime she had only intended to commit.

A detective has placed a target on Jezebel's back, and the time to catch her predator is quickly running out

<u>Savages</u>

An incredibly touching, yet unapologetically brutal trek through a post-apocalyptic wasteland of a civilization that once was.

Two strangers, reliant upon each other for survival face impossible odds, driven by little more than the primitive desire to live, are hunted by vicious hoardes of those who were once human - *savages*...

Mindless and murdering savages. Are they zombies? Are they still human? Whatever the other survivors have become, they no longer speak; they only kill and live like animals.

Parker and Marcus navigate through the ruins and battle through these lingering savages with no answers, searching for the last strain of humanity. Until one discovery changes everything...

The infant's cry shatters their already destroyed world. For Parker, the babe invokes the ghosts of her dead husband and sons. For Iraq war veteran Marcus, the child embodies his hope and gives him innocence to protect. For both, they struggle to determine if faded notions like romance can even still exist in this bleak, dying world.

In this grim post-apocalyptic portrait, the survivors face the horror of not knowing what happened to the world around them as they question whether humanity was ever human at all.

<u>Worship Me</u>

Something is listening to the prayers of St. Paul's United Church, but it's not the god they asked for; it's something much, much older.

A quiet Sunday service turns into a living hell when this ancient entity descends upon the house of worship and claims the congregation for its own. The terrified churchgoers must now prove their loyalty to their new god by giving it one of their children or in two days time it will return and destroy them all.

As fear rips the congregation apart, it becomes clear that if they're to survive this untold horror, the faithful must become the faithless and enter into a battle against God itself. But as time runs out, they discover that true monsters come not from heaven or hell…

…they come from within.

The Big Book of Bootleg Horror 2

The second volume in HellBound Books' flagship horror anthology - this one bursting at the seams with even more fantastically dark horror from the cream of the rising stars in today's horror scene!

Featuring: Tracey A. Cross, Elizabeth Zemlicka, Shelby Thomas, Matthew Gillies, Spinster Eskie, Stephen Clements, Ken Goldman, Nathan Robinson, K.M. Campbell, Cody Grady, Sebastian Bendix, Leo X. Robertson, David Owain Hughes, Timothy McGivney, Kane Gordon, Todd Sullivan, Mike Mayak, Edward Ahern, Rose Garnett, Jaap Boekestein, Brandy Delight, Stanley B. Webb, D. Norfolk, and Thomas Gunther.

Shopping List

A simply superlative collection of spine-tingling horror from the very best minds in the business!

We decided upon the shopping list theme for this particular volume as an antithesis to those wildly successful writers (they know who they are) of whom it is often said *'we would read their damned shopping list if they published it!'*

Well, we have given twenty-one of the hottest authors in the independent horror scene the unique opportunity to have their own shopping lists read by you - along with their most terrifying tales of course!

Stories of gut-wrenching terror from:
Kathy Dinisi, Robert Over, Christopher O'Halloran, Eric W. Burgin, Russ Gartz, Mark Slada, Jeff Baker, Tim Miller, Nick Swain,JC Raye, Jovan Jones, Ben Stevens, David F. Gray, Brandon Cracraft, M.S. Swift, Kevin Holton, David Owain Hughes, Bertram Allan Mullin, Jeff C. Stevenson, Sebastian Crow and S.E. Rise

Demons, Devils and Denizens of Hell Vol, 2

The second volume in HellBound Books' outstanding horror anthology fair teems with tales of Hades' finest citizens – both resident and vacationing in our earthly realm… -

Compiled by the inimitable P. Mattern and featuring: Savannah Morgan, Andrew MacKay, Jaap Boekestein, James H Longmore, Stephanie Kelley, Ryan Woods, James Nichols, P. Mattern, Marcus Mattern, Gerri R Gray, and legion more…

No Rest For The Wicked

A modern day ghost story with its skeletons buried firmly in the past.

From beyond the grave, a murderous wife seeks to complete her revenge on those who betrayed her in life; a powerless domestic still fears for her immortal soul while trying to scare off anyone who comes too close; and the former plantation master - a sadistic doctor who puts more faith in the teachings of de Sade than the Bible When Eric and Grace McLaughlin purchase Greenbrier Plantation, their dreams are just as big as those who have tried to tame the place before them. But, the doctor has learned a thing or two over his many years in the afterlife, is putting those new skills to the test, and will go to great lengths in order to gain the upper hand. While Grace digs into the death-filled history of her new home, Eric soon becomes a pawn of the doctor's unsavory desires and rapidly growing power, and is hell-bent on stopping her.

Blood and Kisses

The definitive short story collecting from James H Longmore - an eclectic mix of dark horror, bizarro and Twilight-Zone style tales of the downright disturbing.

Welcome to the long awaited collection from the writer of horror novels *'Pede* and *Tenebrion*; a forword by Richard Chizmar (co-author of *Gwendy's Button Box* and author of *A Long December*), 18 short stories, 5 flash fiction and even a poem - all skin-crawling, soul-shredding tales of terror, of the darkest things that skulk amongst the night's inky shadows, and of the everyday gone horribly awry.

Discover the alternative implication of technology becoming self-aware, enjoy the acquaintance of a charismatic new pastor who promises his flock a brand new place in which to worship his God, and spend a little time in the company of a nice young man who is inexorably caught up in his home town's terrible secret. Then there is Cupid's revelation that personally he has never experienced love, yet we discover that very emotion alive and not so well amongst the ruins of a post zombie apocalypse world, and we bear witness to a childhood innocence forever destroyed in a war-torn city. There is more, Dear Reader, much, much more; for within these pages we have devils, demons and ghosts, lycanthropes and demi-gods, all rubbing nefarious shoulders with vilest of Hell's offspring who have slithered from the netherworld to doff their caps and wish us all the sweetest of dreams...

**A HellBound Books LLC
Publication**

http://www.hellboundbookspublishing.com

Printed in the United States of America

www.ingramcontent.com/pod-product-compliance
Lightning Source LLC
Chambersburg PA
CBHW060557190726
48283CB00003B/1050